CYCLE of SEASONS
IN
CORRALES

Ruth W. Armstrong

Sunstone Press
Santa Fe, New Mexico

Black and white photographs by Ruth and Ellis Armstrong

Cover photographs by Ellis Armstrong.
Clockwise from upper left:
Rio Grande (Spring)
Corrales Clear Ditch (Summer)
Corrales Clear Ditch (Winter)
Corrales Harvest (Autumn)

First Edition

Printed in the United States of America

Library of Congress Cataloging in Publication Data:

Armstrong, Ruth W.
    Cycle of Seasons in Corrales. / Ruth W. Armstrong. — 1st. ed.
        p.   cm.

    1. Corrales (N.M.) — Description.   2. Corrales (N.M.) — Social life and customs.   3. Seasons
— New Mexico — Corrales. I. Title.
F804.C67A76   1988   88-12232
978.9'57—dc19   CIP
ISBN: 0-86534-124-9 : $8.95

Published in 1988 by SUNSTONE PRESS
                Post Office Box 2321
                Santa Fe, NM 87504-2321 / USA

ℜ

CONTENTS

ꙩꙬ

INTRODUCTION

"In the old days not many people had clocks or watches, so the church bell took their place. It was the Angelus. It rang when it was time to go to the fields, and when it was time to quit. People always knelt for a moment before they left the fields," my friend Mrs. Silva told me.

Most people who live in Corrales today don't wear watches. Corrales is still a pastoral village in spite of the urban tentacles that seek to entwine it every day. Corraleseños haven't changed much through the years, even the newcomers. They love the land, they keep horses, chickens, goats and rabbits. They like to look up and see the Sandias wreathed in clouds, to listen to birds in the bosque, and to eat chili by the bushel.

As Corrales grows and Albuquerque comes closer every day, problems and fears surface. Traffic on the only road through Corrales is bumper-to-bumper morning and evening, and sometimes backed up more than a mile at the intersections approaching Corrales bridge.

The village was incorporated in 1971, so now we cope with taxes and politicians on a more intimate basis than in the past. Maybe two or three hours a day we think about urban problems, but the rest of the time we enjoy our funny little village where we can smell apple blossoms or skunks, mix adobe mud or biscochitos, where people drop whatever they're doing and go help when there's a fire or flood.

Corrales is a microcosm of New Mexico, a curious combination of old and new, sophisticated and earthy, a fairly homogenous blend of people of various races, which has nothing to do with the widely divergent views on almost every subject.

There is a timelessness to Corrales and to New Mexico. What happened four hundred years ago still seems relevant. Days - weeks - centuries pass. Time is part of us, and we of it. Our lives become a time of seasons, more than of numbered years. For us the Angelus still rings.

When the first Spanish entrada established headquarters at Zuni

Pueblo in 1540, Francisco Vasquez de Coronado sent a party ahead to scout the Indian Pueblo country along the Rio Grande. They went across the south end of the malpais to Acoma, then on the old Indian trail to Isleta. On September 7 they reached the river which they called Nuestra Señora and the Indians called P'osage. Here they turned upstream and made camp probably a little south of where Corrales is today.

They were in the midst of the Tiguex Indian Province which extended from Isleta on the south to the pueblos just north and across the river from Bernalillo. There were twelve pueblos in the province, one of which was almost in the center of where Corrales is today.

Captain Hernando de Alvarado, leader of the advance party, sent an envoy carrying a cross to each pueblo, inviting them to come to his camp. The Indians must have been curious to see what kind of creature rode strange beasts, and wore shining hard hats and clothing. Representatives from all twelve pueblos came. Alvarado reported to Coronado: ''They marched around our tent, playing a flute and with an old man for a spokesman. In this manner they came inside the tent and presented me with food, cotton cloth and skins. This river of Nuestra Señora flows through a broad valley planted with fields of maize and dotted with cottonwood groves. The houses are built of mud and are two stories high. The natives seem to be good people, more devoted to agriculture than war. They have a good supply of maize, melons and turkeys in great abundance. They clothe themselves in cotton, the skins of cattle (buffalo) and coats made of turkey feathers, and they wear their hair short.''*

Even after four and a half centuries that description is still accurate enough. There are still wild cottonwood groves along the river which we call the bosque; there are fields of corn, beans and melons, the people are hospitable and more devoted to agriculture than to war. Some have short hair.

The twelve Tiguex Pueblos were abandoned at the time of the Pueblo Revolt in 1680, with most of them going west to live with the Hopis. After the re-conquest they did not return to the pueblo in Corrales, so Spanish history in Corrales began in 1710 with the Alameda Land Grant made to Francisco Montes y Vigil. He was a soldier and officer with de Vargas when New Mexico was reconquered in 1692-94. As was the custom, a land grant was made to Montes y Vigil as payment for his military service. He never settled the grant, however, still being a soldier in the Governor's army, so two years later he sold it to Captain Juan Gonzales, *alcalde* and *Capitán de Guerra* (mayor and war

*(Coronado, Knight of Pueblo and Plains, Herbert Eugene Bolton, UNM Press, 1949, page 184)

captain), chief military and civil officer at Bernalillo.

This area was already called "Corrales" because corrals had been built for horses of the Spanish soldiers who were stationed on the west side of the river to protect settlers and Pueblo Indians from Navajos who swooped down from the west to raid on the east side of the river. Capt. Gonzales built an adobe hacienda in the south end of Corrales, farmed the valley land and ran sheep on the mesa. He sold part of the grant to friends from Bernalillo, the Gutierrez family, who built a house near where the old church stands today. Another part was sold to the Martinez family whose hacienda was where the Casa Viejo Restaurant is today, and the northern part of the grant was sold to the Montoyas, another powerful family from Bernalillo. That part came to be called Corrales Alto or Upper Corrales. The Gonzales Rancho was known as Corrales Abajo or Lower Corrales. Today we call it Baja Corrales.

The character of people in New Mexican villages like Corrales was set in the 1700's, a character so deeply ingrained that in some ways it has not changed much. Time stood still in the eighteenth century. Spain was a waning world power, and maintained the poor province of New Mexico in the most minimal way, only from a sense of responsibility to the settlers who had stuck it out, and to the thousands of Pueblo Indians who had been Christianized. The great period of expansion and mission-building had ended with the rebellion. Communication was slow, it took up to three years to get a letter to and an answer from the mother country, so the people here learned to depend on themselves and each other. No one had money, business was by barter of goods and services. People learned to make-do or do without. Only a very few knew how to read and write. The *ricos*, the *gente de razon*, sons and grandsons of the conquistadors, owned large tracts of land. Around them gathered the paisanos, men of the soil, who received protection, food and shelter in exchange for work in the fields, houses and with the livestock. The eighteenth and early nineteenth centuries in New Mexico were the nearest thing to a feudal society that every existed in this country. The earliest settlements in Corrales were part of this system.

Not many people in Corrales make a living by farming anymore, but almost everyone has a garden and a few animals. There is a strong feeling of family and interdependence. Any excuse is good enough for a fiesta, just like in the old days. San Ysidro, patron saint of farmers, is the patron saint of Corrales, and a fiesta honoring him is still held every May.

Corrales is only twelve miles from the Big Eye, that maze of steel and concrete where Interstates 40 and 25 meet in downtown Albuquerque. Twelve miles isn't much as the crow flies and many do but it is a journey from one world to another, from urban life in a pleasant western city, to the wild natural bosque of cottonwood and Russian olive trees along the Rio Grande. Here coyotes den and raise their pups, beavers cut down trees, birds by the thousands nest and others follow the Rio Grande like a highway from nesting grounds in the north to winter feeding grounds in the south, and vice versa. The bosque may have been like this when Coronado marched through in 1541; when Oñate led the first permanent settlers north in 1598. It may have even been like this when Ice Age man crouched under the brow of the volcanic escarpment waiting for game to go toward the river. Maybe it has been this lush only since the Conservancy drained the bogs with a network of ditches beginning in 1929.

Whether it has changed or not, the bosque conveys a sense of history, of timelessness. I feel a comradeship with others who have walked along the Rio Grande — nomadic Indians, Pueblo Indians, farmers, hunters, conquistadors, padres, settlers in oxcarts, traders on the Chihauhua Trail, herders driving sheep or cattle, covered wagon pioneers, homesteaders, miners, latter-day pioneers driving cars and trucks to California — with everyone who has traversed this land and been refreshed by the river and the trees.

At the south end of Corrales a narrow foot bridge goes across Riveside Drain to the bosque. No matter what the season I can look out the window and see fishermen, birdwatchers, walkers, horseback riders, and joggers along the edge of the bosque, and walk there often, myself.

Nothing is more serene than walking in the bosque after a fresh-fallen snow. I like to make the first tracks. The air is cold and brittle, and if I brush against a branch, I cause a new snowstorm.

I like to walk along the ditches on snowy nights, too, usually a time to be guaranteed solitude. One time was an exception. I heard muffled footsteps and saw a figure before it came even with me on the opposite side of the ditch. It was a man, bent slightly into the falling snow, walking steadily and purposefully. Within a few minutes he was swallowed up into the grey shadows of the bosque. I knew somehow, that he was a wetback who has stayed into the winter finishing a harvesting job in Corrales. The snow came sooner than expected and he was hurrying toward the warmth of Mexico.

In the spring the bosque is laden with the sweet fragrance of Russian olive blossoms, not much bigger than a pinhead, but so many millions they drench the bosque with perfume. In summer it is a shady, lazy retreat, and in the fall the cottonwoods form a golden umbrella.

There is a cleared area in the bosque that is cared for by druids, I think. I have never seen anyone there, but it always has the feeling that someone just left, and will come back as soon as I leave. Logs and stumps form a circle around a place where they probably dance in the light of the full moon. There is never any trash there, and seldom any footprints.

I have found another secret place farther north along the bank of the river. An arbor has been built in the thick willows on the bank, and a metal grate is there to cook fish or whatever they bring with them. I never distrub anything. It is their secret — and mine.

I count myself lucky to have lived on the edge of the bosque for twenty-nine years, watching wild things grow, bloom and sing. Day flows into week, week into month and month into year, so beautiful it makes my heart ache. Every day I look at the Sandias and I am glad, not just for these — my mountains, but for all the mountains, plains, deserts, arroyos, blades of grass and people that make up this place called New Mexico. I'm grateful to my parents for coming to New Mexico before I was born, and to my mother who looked at the plains, mesas and mountains of New Mexico while she was pregnant, and in some mystical way transmitted her love of this state to the embryo she was carrying.

Corrales is the essence of New Mexico. We have the rich and the poor, Spaniards and Chicanos, Jews and gentiles, Catholics and Protestants, ditch diggers, farmers and professors.

I have watched more than the seasons come and go. Characters and setting flow smoothly in a warm, gentle stream. The years have melded together in a calendar that goes back to the forgotten past, and forward to the unguessable. It is a hoop snake calendar — tail in mouth, no beginning and no end. Everything is in relation to the time of year — when the hummers come, when the leaves turn, when the cranes fly over. Every event, major or routine, is woven into memories of the dramatic environment where it happened, a day on the calendar in this suburban wilderness.

*(Coronado, Knight of Pueblo and Plains, Herbert Eugene Bolton, UNM Press, 1949, page 184)

JANUARY. *Corrales Riverside Drain.*

JANUARY

Time of the Strong Cold

We like our winter sunshine in New Mexico, but the winter days I like best are damp and grey. They give me a snug, private feeling. In the field next to ours stands the tallest cottonwood tree in Corrales. Standing alone as it does, it gets all the food, water and sunshine that would be divided among dozens of trees if it were surrounded by the rest of the bosque. On a soft, grey January morning the field is often covered with ground fog swirling around the big cottonwood tree. Horses and cows standing below it appear and disappear like ghosts in a mystical scene.

The ground is warmer than the air, so it creates a mist that will be gone as soon as the sun warms the air. On such a January day the Sandias might as well not be there, so hidden are they by clouds and fog. But the clouds drop their snow and move on, leaving the mountains white all the way to the bottom. In late afternoon the sun comes out, etching sharp black and white lines around every boulder on the craggy, worn western face of the Sandias. As the cold winter sun nears the horizon the mountains turn fluorescent pink, like a strawberry sundae with marshmallow topping. The Sandias put on a show all times of year, but in winter lines are sharper, colors more startling. There's nothing shy about New Mexico colors. They usually tend to be overdone. Where a nice pastel pink might do somewhere else, here it will be hot pink, even if it's on snow.

The crows come by almost every afternoon. Early in the morning they fly over going north, but seldom stop, in a hurry to get to the cropped grain fields and the big dairy at the north end of the village. In late afternoon they fly a few miles south again. Hundreds light in our field, like ink spots on tan velvet; hundreds more swoosh through the trees. They remind me of the Alfred Hitchcock movie, *Birds*. Everytime I look up there are more there - big black glossy bodies, making a terrible racket. If I go outside it disturbs them and they fly to another tree, but they keep swarming like bees between field and trees in our yard and across the ditch in the bosque.

A few individuals fly about on their own, but mostly they move as a flock. They sit awhile, walk up and down limbs, talk to each other, and drive the cats crazy. If the cats were outside they would slink toward cover, but inside the house they are brave, and sit in the window with chins quivering and tails twitching.

I've heard that crows communicate with at least four different calls, and post lookouts while the main body of the flock feeds. I'm not sure. About the time I see one acting like a lookout, he flies down and joins the group, but they do make at least four different calls, none of which I have decoded.

When we lived in town I used to see the crows make their popcorn run almost every morning when I was hanging diapers on the clothesline. We lived on their flight pattern between two drive-in theaters where they cleaned up popcorn from the night before. Every morning they flew over from south to north just like they do in Corrales.

I enjoy the winter birds more than the summer ones. They are friendlier, have more time to entertain us, and spend a lot more time on the seed feeder. They're not in a hurry to go somewhere else, to build a nest, and they're not raising families. They just eat and sing, or in the case of the crows, shriek, caw and gargle.

Sometimes in January a flock of fifty or more robins comes through, descending on the birdbath and feeder. It's hard to know if these are late going south, or early going north. There is such a short time between the last of the south-going robins and the first of the north-goers, they never seem to be gone.

At any time of year a swift shaft of bright orange through the bare trees tells me the flickers are here. Black and white feathers drift downward; the rat-a-tat of their beaks drills into half-dead tree trunks. On the ground they kick at the dry leaves, stirring up a small hurricane, and poke their long beaks into the soft ground looking for bugs and ants.

Juncos or snow birds, house finches and sparrows are our regular boarders all winter. Juncos are the smallest and most obstreperous of the three. They chase each other across the seed feeder, but the chasee simply flies up and comes down again at the other end of the feeder, and chases the one in front of him. They sit on the bare limbs above the feeder, quickly dart down and eat a few seeds, and return to the tree. They peck at one seed at a time, nibble it gently, drop the hull and swallow the kernel, just like an experienced New

Mexican eats piñons.

We put out more seeds several times a day, and by the time we get back inside the house the feeder is covered with birds again. A nuthatch darts in, grabs a sunflower seed and hustles back to the cottonwood tree where he runs up and down the trunk. A chickadee walks across the bottom of the feeder — upside down — and over the edge to peck at a seed or two. There is often a towhee with the juncos, looking like a big brother to the Oregon junco.

On those January mornings when it has snowed during the night, I like to walk early. If it's a light snow it will disappear as soon as the sun touches it, leaving the ground soft and fragrant, but the air stays colder than the water in the ditch, and mist swirls above it in the weak sunlight. Frost touches the pink bare limbs of the willows. The last few drops of melted frost on bushes turns to sparkling diamonds.

Jasmine would be a good state flower. On more than one January morning I have looked out the window to see jasmine blooming through snow. If I clip a few stalks and put them in water, little yellow blossoms will appear the next day on what looked like a dead stick. Jasmine is tough, persistent, takes no care and likes the environment. Branches grow at angles that have little pattern, and it blooms earlier than almost any other plant. Its blossoms are a contrast to the ungainly stems. It is a plant of courage and individuality, like New Mexico. It fits here.

Superbowl Sunday has come to be a special January event in the neighborhood. Someone has a dinner or a potluck, we make up pools for the score at the end of each quarter and the game, so everyone goes home, if not a winner, at least well-fed and content. It's not so much a matter of caring who wins, it's just a matter of getting with friends.

Nora and Bryan Johnson have hosted more than their share of Superbowl parties because they have several televisions and fireplaces, and also Nora makes the best green chili in Corrales. Every fall they make a several-day event out of roasting nine or ten bushels of green chile on the outside grill, and freezing it. It's a lot of work in October, but oh! how good it tastes in January!

Last year we walked home from the Superbowl party at Johnsons just before dark, as big fat snowflakes began to fall. The smell of burning logs in fireplaces wafted across the snow-covered ground, and a great hush held the land. Our tummies were full of green chili. God was in His heaven, and all was right with the world.

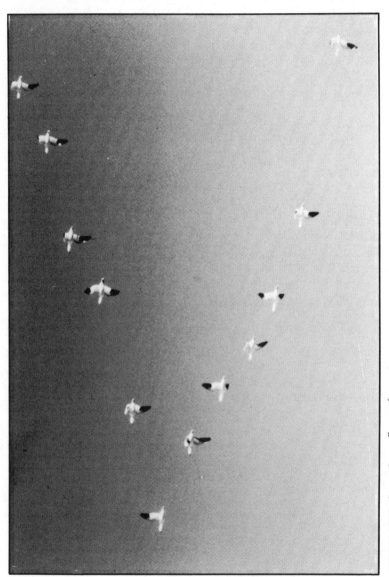

FEBRUARY. *Snow Geese fly north.*

᳞

FEBRUARY

When Birds Go North

Flocks of sandhill cranes and snow geese are already going north, though the days are still cold. Long streamers of gray shift and swirl against the cold blue sky, sometimes in formation, headed due north, sometimes circling uncertainly. Once in a while with the sandhills will be a whooper, its big white body contrasting with the pearl gray of the sandhills. There is no mistaking the whooper — his wingspan is about ninety inches, almost a foot more than the sandhill. Flocks of snow geese and Canada geese fly over too, but we seldom see them except when the snow geese land in a field for a snack, or the Canadas land on an island in the river.

Even after all these years I cannot watch a flock of geese or cranes go overhead without feeling a surge of loneliness, as if they were abandoning me. Is it an urge born in the mists of man's primeval past when he lived wherever instinct took him, when he followed game, when he knew no laws but the sure and unforgiving laws of nature? Even the most urbanized city dweller reacts in some way to the call of the wild cranes and geese. Man has not been on this earth yet long enough to be entirely free of primitive urges, but he's trying.

Sometime in February we always have a false spring. Newcomers spade up garden plots and start poring over seed catalogues, but it is a waste of time. Winter is not through with us yet. Even though I know false spring is only a teaser, as transitory as a two-year-old's attention span, it is a joy. Somedays it is possible to turn off the heat and leave the doors open. The Game and Fish Department stocks the ditches with trout and all ages and denominations of fishermen come out to soak up the sun. Belted kingfishers fly up and down the ditch, lighting on branches and wires above the ditch to cock a keen eye on the water below. I wonder if Game and Fish knows who catches a lot of their fish? Fat brown muskrats turn sommersaults in the clear water, looking for some goody buried in the muck on the bottom.

False spring may last a week, then, sure enough, winter comes again. Skiers know they have several more weeks of fun. Given the week of encouragement the jasmine finishes what it brazenly started in January, bursting out along bare twigs with thousands of little yellow blossoms. A few birds return in February, noisily discussing the real estate situation. Far above I see an arrow of geese pointing north, so high and swift only a faint, fleeting honk reaches me. How different these creatures of the stratosphere are from the raucous crows strutting on the branches of olive trees, gorging on the dried seeds, from the thousands of starlings that pepper the bare cottonwood branches.

I remember Sophie — she loved to sit in the sun during February's false spring, her back against the warm wall of her old adobe house. Sophie never married, and she lived alone in a little house close to where she was born. Her family had been in Corrales many generations. An irrigation ditch ran behind Sophie's house, and she carried water by the bucket to water her flowers. For years she was content without indoor plumbing, but progress came to Corrales. In homes of her friends and in homes where she worked, she grew accustomed to automatic appliances, tiled bathrooms, and yards that were watered by hoses or sprinklers. Her friends felt she was getting past the age where she should wade through snow to an outdoor privy, so they got together and decided to build her a new bathroom and install indoor plumbing in the kitchen.

The project delighted and fascinated Sophie. She doubted that the "cessy pool" was all it was cracked up to be, but she was willing to give it a try. The business-like swish of the toilet filled her with pride, and the automatic hot water heater in the kitchen was a marvel.

Her friends gave her a surprise bathroom-warming so they could share her pleasure. When she fingered the new towels and smelled the lotions and powder, words wouldn't come, but her eyes spoke. She took them on a tour to see the improvements. She flushed the toilet and explained that it went to the "cessy" pool. She turned on the hot water tap and had each guest feel it to prove it was really hot. She took them outside to the faucet near the back door where she had a hose attached to water the flowers.

"I'll bet your flowers won't be near as nice as when you watered them with ditch water," said one of her friends.

"Well, maybe not," said Sophie philosophically, "but you know how it is. You get one thing, you gotta get six more."

The first few years we lived in Corrales, we spent a lot of time cleaning up fallen trees and brush from the woods in our yard. In the natural bosque — which our yard was part of — the trees grow close together, and the trunks don't get large like they do where a tree grows alone. Usually they grow to be only a foot or two in diameter, and often the trunks go up twenty or thirty feet before they put our branches. This makes them top-heavy, and since cottonwoods tend to be brittle anyway, when there's a stiff wind one or two come crashing down. When we moved there there was a lot of wood on the ground and more kept accumulating. It was a fire hazard as we found out one year, so we decided we had to do something about it. Our own wood pile got higher than we could reach, so we decided to share.

We put up a sign on the highway saying "Free Wood", and people started coming right away, but always looked surprised when we showed them a whole log and gave them a saw. Most people would cut up at least part of a log, but some didn't make an effort to cut up any at all. Those were the ones we watched as they drove past our wood pile. No one ever came back for a second load. So much for free wood!

But we found out, that first February in Corrales, that people would work a lot harder for a dog than a cord of wood. The first thing we got after we moved to Corrales was a beautiful black and silver German Shepherd dog, the best breed of "working dog" known to man. Soon after we got her, Queenie (Dame Marie aus Christy) came into season. This opened up a whole new vocabulary and field of thought for the children, especially the eight-year-old. Any dog that didn't carry on like Queenie was "out of season;" any curious male dog that came around was interested in "bread." I kept a close eye on Queenie, but when we had to be gone we locked her up in the chicken house, an adobe building with cement floors, and a high window over which we nailed one-by-sixes.

Queenie had a boyfriend named Sheriff (Baku of Cedarhurst), also a German shepherd, weighing in at ninety pounds. One day when I was gone to the grocery store, Sheriff working from the outside and Queenie from the inside managed to tear off all the boards, and had themselves a honeymoon.

In due time eight pups were born, on a December night when snow and the barometer were falling fast. Both sides of our in-laws had arrived for our first holidays in Corrales. We had planned to go to a party that night, but cancelled it to help Queenie through labor. We made her comfortable out in the garage, close to the house.

The first three weeks about all I had to do was change the straw in their bed every day, and cook for Queenie who was ravenous. I fed and watered her several times a day, but her pans were always empty.

January came and still the weather was bitter cold, and going out to take care of the dogs meant bundling up in heavy clothing. At three weeks their weaning began. It took only two or three days to teach the pups to lap milk and broth from a bowl, but those two or three days are etched into my memory, and I began to realize that whoever had named these a working breed, weren't necessarily referring to the dogs. I began by spoon feeding each one five time a day. Multiply five by eight, by five minutes per feeding, and you will see how much time was left. They had to have more room so we moved them out to the chicken house where it had all started.

The next four weeks were a blur of cooking hot cereal with raw eggs in it, meat and vegetable broth, bouillon and other nutritious food for them. These were dogs with good pedigrees, you see, and we had to treat them as such. At least Queenie had had the good judgement to pick a mate with as good a pedigree as hers.

The chicken house was about a football field's length from the house, so I spent most of February running through the snow with pots of steaming barley soup and hot water to melt the ice on their drinking pans.

Finally came the day we put an ad in the paper to sell them, and then I learned the full definition of "working dogs." We advertised the pups by saying we would trade them for work on the house. We thought that anyone willing to work for a puppy would be a good owner. We could have traded twice the number of pups. We got a new roof on the new addition, all the outside trim painted, new formica cabinet tops and some bricks laid. We gave one as a seeing-eye dog, kept one, and traded six. One woman wanted to do housework for one, but I couldn't afford to "spend" them that way. We got the work done, the pups got good homes, and the new owners got fine registered German shepherd pups without spending any cash, one of our smartest ventures.

Queenie was not cut out for suburban living. She petrified the meter reader, salesmen, bill collectors and friends, so we gave her to some friends who had a ranch in Oregon, far away from people. Baron, the pup we kept, was a big, quiet, loveable dog who was stolen when he was almost grown. We searched for weeks, but never found him. He is the only pet I remember crying for since I was a child. Sam was another one from the litter. He was big and friendly, black and silver like his mother, and had been "bought" by a man who put on most of the new roof. He had to leave town and asked us to take Sam back, but Sam developed a taste for fresh meat. First it was chickens.

He killed all three of our bantams, and though we wired a dead carcass around his neck, and he was so embarrased he would not look us in the eye, it didn't break him of the habit. Next it was pork. By this time we had Sally, a young German shepherd female, and Sam led her astray. One day a neighbor told us that both dogs had gotten into his field and were chasing down a young pig. He shot and killed Sally, but Sam escaped. We knew Sam was the guilty party, not Sally, but we couldn't blame the neighbor too much. We kept Sam penned up for several weeks, a miserable thing to do to a big German shepherd who had enjoyed complete freedom up to then. But he eventually got out and went to another neighbor's and ran down a young lamb. The vet patched up the lamb, we paid the bill, and found a home for Sam elsewhere.

MARCH. Indian rock art on the escarpment near Corrales. Was the one on the
right made after bearded Europeans had entered tiquex?

ℐℰ

MARCH

Time of the New Bud

March weather is as unpredictable as a thirteen-year-old girl's love life. If I ever leave New Mexico it will be during a bad windstorm in March. Here in the bosque we're sheltered by the trees, but that's not enough when the wind comes howling out of the west, pushing weeds, paper and sand before it like an ugly, dirty brute. I put my hands over my ears and turn up the radio, and by night I feel emotionally drained, as if I had been fighting with someone all day. The wind, too, usually spends its strength by nightfall, but on those nights when it continues to blow, it can really drive a sane person mad.

Then along comes a March day so gentle and sweet it tears your heart out. I remember a day like that one year, so benign and fresh I couldn't sit at the typewriter, so I decided to go see the petroglyphs on the volcanic escarpment between Paradise Hills and Taylor Ranch. I hadn't been there for a dozen years, not since I helped the New Mexico Archaeological Society record all the petroglyphs in the Albuquerque area. I was working at the Chamber of Commerce then, but every Sunday I went over to the escarpment by myself and worked a few hours. It was always quiet; never once in nine months was I disturbed by another soul. At that time Taylor Ranch didn't exist, and not many souls lived in Paradise Hills. Coors Boulevard was a two-lane country road.

When I began the project I didn't know a pictograph from a petroglyph, but it didn't take a scientist to do what I did. I was assigned the mile and half of escarpment immediately south of Paradise Boulevard. All I was required to do was draw a rough sketch of each location (usually a canyon or recess into the escarpment), put a ruler alongside each petroglyph or group of petroglyphs and take a black and white picture of it. On another sheet of paper I was to describe each numbered petroglyph as it looked to me. These descriptions were more creative than scientific, such as "rabbit-eared kachina", "man with arrow through head", "snake with horns", "dancer with bent knees", "four-legged animal". It was as much fun as taking an ink blot test. Whatever came to mind I could put down, and it was surprising how the experts could take my photos and descriptions and come up with identification.

The petroglyphs tended to be in clusters on sunny canyons into the escarpment, and we were asked to name the areas too. My territory included four major canyons: Metate, Kissing Bird, Atl-Atl and Handprint Canyons. We members of the Society turned in our papers and pictures to archaeologists at the Laboratory of Anthropology in Santa Fe, and there they remain today, I suppose, available to anyone who wants to study them.

One Sunday I found something really exciting - a large, fairly smooth lava rock, tilted back like the side of a triangle. On it were carved only a cross and the date 1541. I thought from the weathering it looked more than fifty or a hundred years old. It seemed too sophisticated a hoax for an early day sheep herder to have thought of, so I thought it might be a grave marker for one of the Franciscan priests who were here with the Coronado Expedition in 1540-41. They had headquartered at an Indian Pueblo near Bernalillo, and must have traveled up and down the Rio Grande. But alas! We called in an expert geologist and an anthropologist and after much scrutiny with a magnifying glass and a study of the style of numerals, they concluded it was not four hundred years old, but couldn't pinpoint the date any closer than that. I liked my version better.

The petroglyph survey was one of the pleasantest projects I ever worked on, and I saw a fair amount of wildlife. One day I saw either a small mountain lion or the biggest wildcat in Bernalillo County. It was four or five feet from nose to tail, and disappeared soundlessly into a rocky, weedy crevice. One time I saw a beautiful red fox, another a tawny tomcat that had wandered over from Paradise Hills. One morning I stepped on a sleepy bull snake, but it was a while before I got up nerve enough to go back and see for *sure* that it was a bull snake.

Crouching below the rim of a headland of the escarpment Sunday after Sunday I began to think like early man. I could easily imagine I was crouched there watching the river valley for signs of deer or bison, or even a mammoth. As I waited I passed the time by scratching a picture on the smooth volcanic surface behind me. I made a picture of three tiny antelopes, and through one's heart I etched a spear. The gods would know this was my prayer for good hunting. I returned to this same place year after year, and each time I etched the picture a little deeper into the stone. After I died other hunters continued to scratch away at my picture until it was as deep as a finger. Then my people quit following the game, and my picture sat there watching the valley for hundreds of years, until some man with a sledgehammer knocked it loose to take it home to his rock garden. But it broke and he threw it away on the mesa.

It was a shock and a disappointment to me, that lovely March day when I revisited the petroglyphs, to see how much vandalism had been done in twelve years. Many petroglyphs had been carried away, big rocks blasted apart to break off the picture someone wanted for their garden or fireplace, and almost all had been damaged in target shooting. These primitive forms of art and communication had endured hundreds, maybe thousands of years, adding an imperceptable layer of desert varnish each year, and in one decade they had been destroyed.

When we did the rock art survey we tried to get "my" area set aside as a state park since it contained the best, the most, and the most varied petroglyphs on the entire escarpment, but Horizon Land Corporation could never quite make up its mind to give the land. D.W. Falls, however, developer of Volcano Cliffs, was willing to dedicate part of the escarpment on his land, and Petroglyph State Park was established, so at least those petroglyphs have been preserved, while many of those near Paradise Hills are ruined.

As distasteful as I find March winds, the month does have a lot going for it. Buds appear, ready to burst with the slightest encouragement. Flickers and woodpeckers are busy tattooing trees, brown creepers and nuthatches run up and down tree trunks any direction, any end up, listening for worms in the bark. The juncos disappear around the first of the month, but the robins come back by the dozens, fluttering and splashing in the birdbath and at the edge of the ditches. The ditch water is low and clear in early spring, perfect for a good bath after a long trip.

New robins have to learn about window glass. They fly into it so hard they leave a clump of feathers sticking to the glass. After such an encounter they fly up to a branch, fluff their feathers, stare into space for a while, probably wondering why they have such a headache. The cats are fascinated. They sit open-mouthed on window sills, enjoying the robin show, but not caring to go outside. A few laggard flocks of geese and cranes fly over, in no hurry to catch the others who have been going north for six weeks.

One early March morning I saw three coyotes trotting along the bank on the other side of the ditch. The two pups and one adult looked like small tan and brown shepherd dogs. That explained the yapping we had heard a few times on quiet winter nights. We imagined the scene that took place those nights: the pups had kept absolutely still while their mother hunted, but when she returned with fresh meat they set up an excited yapping, which stopped suddenly as they got their share of dinner.

Now, on that bright March morning, I imagined the mother coyote was telling the pups they were old enough to leave the nest. She trotted north on the levee with the pups at her heels. Suddenly she wheeled and ran the opposite direction faster than the pups could run, and disappeared into the bosque.

March is the perfect time of year to hike the trails on the west side of the Sandias, not too hot, not too cold. The waterfall in Waterfall Canyon is still frozen and ice climbers can climb it. On the stream below, the ice forms just a shimmering film like cellophane on the water. Pussywillows along the bank are beginning to sprout tiny fairy kittens on the bare stalks.

March is the time to start thinking about a garden, but not to plant it. Maybe rototill and fertilize it, but not to plant it. Our garden is in a field north of the house which was a narrow strip of land we bought after we bought the rest of the property. This was part of the Garcia Strip which ran from the river to the *ceja* or brow of the mesa. It was ten years from the time we first approached the Garcias until they sold it to us. When the family dwindled to one elderly man with no children, he remembered our offer.

The Garcia Strip is a good example of much of the land in New Mexico, and especially in agricultural villages like Corrales. The strip is only one to two hundred feet wide, and about two miles long, the last remnant of a land grant that reached from river to mountains or mesa as all land grants did. As parents died, and divided land among children, they tried to guarantee that each one retained access to the water and to grazing or timber land. With each generation the strips of land became narrower, creating some pretty unusual looking property maps today, and lots of headaches for title companies.

Most irrigable and grazing land in New Mexico was granted by the King of Spain to early settlers. There were two kinds of land grants: large private grants containing thousands of acres, made to individuals who had helped with the settlement, and the community land grants. These latter were made when as many as thirty families petitioned the King for permission to start a new settlement. They were given communal lands for grazing, wood chopping, communal water rights, and each family had land for farming. As long as the grantees or their heirs remained on the land, it was theirs, but they never had title to it, and if they moved away, it reverted to the crown. With communication what it was in the 1700s and early 1800s, ownership was often uncertain and controversial in many cases, relying on memory and tradition rather than written records.

So every year when we plant our little garden on the Garcia Strip, we feel we have a connection with the ancient system of land use in New Mexico.

I can't count the number of dogs that have been dumped on us. One March morning I heard little whimpers near the ditch which turned out to be a box full of puppies not more than a month old. We kept them until they were big enough to give away, but we let our youngest child keep one. Gus turned out to be about the best dog we ever had. He was part collie, black and glossy, with tan spots above his eyes that gave him look of perpetual surprise. Margy was in her Four H phase at the time, so she took him through obedience training as her project. Came the day for the dog show and the whole family turned out to watch Margy put Gus through his paces. He did fairly well with all the commands, but he was not really a serious dog, and thought the whole affair was a social event. One by one the awards were handed out, but nothing came to Gus until the last one, created on the spot, we suspected, by kind judges. He won the tail wagging contest.

There were many other dogs, but Rina outlasted them all. She was a little black cocker spaniel, a stray our daughter picked up on the University of New Mexico campus. We had her fourteen years. When the daughter was married, part of the deal was that the groom got Rina too, but she wasn't happy living in town, and became a very insecure little dog, slinking around the perimeter of a room, not having the courage to walk across it. So we took her back, and she spent many happy years chasing butterflies and lying in the sun. The last few months of her life she became weak and sick, and often stood still for ten or fifteen minutes, staring off through the trees, surely remembering the days she had romped through the woods and along the ditchbank with the kids. They were all gone, it was quiet now, she was old and ready to lie down and die. I probably waited a day or two too long, but I had to be sure. When I was, I took her to the vet and had her put to sleep, and brought her home and buried her in the woods about a hundred feet from the front door.

We have had twenty to thirty cats, more if you count kittens. Omar Khayyam was a beautiful blue point Siamese, who was Uncle Ky to several generations of kittens. Pardo was a slate-grey-and-white tabby who had to have her kittens by cesarean section. Licorice was a sweet old ordinary black-and-white tomcat who waited for our son after school, obviously relishing the game of jumping out at him from behind a bush.

Madam (she loved to entertain tomcats) was one of the strangest. All one cold winter I caught glimpses of her scrawny, ugly little body tiptoeing through the woods and snow toward an abandoned beaver den in the ditch bank where I assumed she lived. If we made the slightest noise, she disappeared in a flash. I began putting food out at night which was always gone in the morning, but she wouldn't get within a hundred feet of us. One warm March morning I had the doors open, and heard a tiny mewing on the upstairs deck. There were three kittens crawling out from the space between roof and deck. Naturally I petted them, so that afternoon Madam moved them out to the beaver den. It was an exhausting job for a small mother cat to jump from roof to viga to buttress to ground. She would carry a kitten a few feet, then lay it down to rest a bit, but eventually she had them all moved.

A week or so later our neighbor brought over one kitten he had rescued when he found a dog digging into the den. We assumed the other two were dead. I put this one in a box in the garage, and next day was surprised to see Madam's beady eyes staring suspiciously at me from behind some stacked boxes. She had brought the other two kittens into the garage. Frightened of people as she was, she still knew she and her kittens were safer with us than in the beaver den.

After three quick litters of kittens, Madam was completely gentled. She became a fat, thick-furred, affectionate but stand-offish cat. The slightest noise sends her running. Only true cat lovers ever find her appealing, because she never does anything to make herself endearing. Friendship is on her snooty terms if at all. She can usually be counted on to get into the lap of the one person in the room who despises cats.

Kittens, puppies, apricot trees — everything seems to bud out in March, in spite of the uncertainty of the weather. Dark and dreary one minute, sunny the next, clouds white against a cobalt sky. Then the curtain closes again, and black bottoms of the clouds form a low ceiling. Sometimes rain falls steadily and silently, except for an occasional growl of thunder, an alien sound in March. Toward the end of March there is usually a hard, wet snow. Nighttime temperatures drop to single digits in the valley, and any buds that have appeared are doomed.

APRIL. *The house in Corrales where we moved in 1959.*

⤳ℭ

APRIL

Green Up Time

When I hear the sad cool call of the mourning dove I know Spring is near. A flood of memories washes over me as I recall the April we bought the house in Corrales. The call of the dove, more than any other sound, brings it all back.

Right from the beginning I knew the place was charmed, not haunted but charmed. We signed the papers one bright beguiling April Fool's Day, and two weeks later moved in. It is those two weeks that the cry of the dove brings back.

Our friends in the northeast heights thought we were crazy. Banks wouldn't finance anything in Corrales then; it was a twelve mile drive from town, and the only way across the river was a narrow, dangerous bridge. Everyone said: 1. our kids would drown in the ditches; 2. we'd never get our money out of it; 3. for the same price we could have bought a brand new split level Mankin Stardust home in the HEIGHTS, for heaven's sake. Instead we took on an adobe house that wasn't new enough to have good wiring or plumbing, nor old enough to have tradition. It wasn't even livable.

But it was foreordained that we buy this place. About twelve years earlier when Ellis was teaching at the Seventh Day Adventist Academy in Corrales, he used to stop for coffee with Grace and Harvey Caplin who had moved to Corrales in 1947. He often took their mutt, Tuffy, for a walk, and told me about "a nice clearing in the bosque behind Caplins that would be just right for a house." So it was, but someone else bought it and built a house. Now here we were in April, 1959, buying it from them.

Those people had known sorrow, separation, divorce, sickness, disappointment and death in this house. The ghosts were still alive. Frustration and anger had been vented on the house, and a pall of sadness hung over it. Neighbors told me the woman had fallen in love with a younger man, and taken the children and left. The husband, they said, drank himself to death in a few months. I found parts of letters that made me feel as if I were watching the drama. Every room had broken glass in it, usually near the wall heater. I could see him finishing a bottle, and in hurt and anger throwing it at the heater. Grills and knobs were broken off the heaters. The patio was carpeted with broken glass. The dark red cement floor was caked with blood, vomit, grease and dirt. On hands and knees I scrubbed every square inch of it with steel wool, using a putty knife to loosen hard globs. As I removed the dirt I removed the ghosts, and day by day the house became ours.

The house had been vacant for almost a year, tied up in probate court, and had been taken over by intruders. Campers had built fires in the middle of the living room floor. Plumbing was ruined, the roof leaked, window panes were broken, door locks had been pried off. The real estate agent had nailed all doors shut with six inch spikes, ruining the frames.

In spite of these drawbacks, we were still elated about our big house in Corrales. I didn't feel repulsion at the filth, only sorry for the people who had built and loved and lost this house. Their children had scratched their names in foot-high letters on an outside wall, and when I scrubbed them with a wire brush, the lightened letters were left on the wall forever. It was their attempt to tell the world "I live here. This is my house." They were gone, their father was dead, their mother had a new husband. So much for a child's dreams of security and home.

Little by little the house shaped up. During those two weeks, orchestrated to the call of the mourning doves, the house and bosque became familiar and dear. Every day the leaves grew a tiny bit greener, wild asparagus began to poke green spears through the dirt. Birds were building nests and telling the whole world about it. The weather was warm and sweet, and the doors were wide open so the bosque came inside with me.

We moved in on a Saturday. I had taken out bits and pieces every day, but on Saturday we made the final move with the big things. The kids loved the space and freedom. We worked hard all day, got most everything in place, and had supper on the floor in front of the fireplace where the fire took the chill off the spring evening. We fell into bed, exhausted and happy, each of us dreaming his own dreams about a new life in a big adobe house in the country.

Before midnight someone hammered on the front screen. We both went to the door and there stood a disheveled middle-aged couple, a little muddy, wanting to use our phone to call the sheriff. They had been parked on the ditch, they said, when someone rolled them, took his wallet and the car. We felt sorry for them, and sat drinking coffee with them until the sheriff arrived.

We became hardened to such tales of woe, however, after they happened almost every Saturday night until the frost was on the pumpkin. The stories were never quite the same. Sometimes they backed their car into the ditch and wanted us to pull them out; sometimes their car wouldn't start; sometimes they were out of gas, or their friends had gone off and left them. We eventually got to where we could say, "Sorry. There's a phone two miles up the road."

We not only had to reclaim the house but the five acres around it too. It was unbelievable the liberties people took with the property because it had been abandoned for a year. One Sunday morning we got up to find a family of four camped in our yard, not a hundred feet from the front door, cooking eggs over an open fire. Another time when I asked a group to put out a bonfire that was sending flames dangerously close to the cottonwood limbs, they said "We been building fires here a long time."

One Saturday night we came home late to find a carload of teenagers sitting around a bonfire in the middle of our driveway — burning our sign that said "Private Property."

I'll never forget the time I walked to the mailbox about ten in the morning. Halfway down the driveway I saw a pair of girl's panties hanging on a tree branch. Under the tree were a couple pretty interested in each other. I coughed and walked past them to the mailbox, but was too embarrassed to come back, so I went on down the road to Caplin's and waited until we saw their car go by. But for every such unpleasant event there were a dozen good ones. With a little perspective even the unpleasant ones got to be funny.

The nicest thing that happened to me during the time I was putting the ghosts to rest and reclaiming the house was meeting Louie Chavez. Occasionally I looked up from my scrubbing to see this tall, greying, handsome man walking along the fence that divided our property from the Garcia Strip. I would nod and continue my painting/scrubbing/scraping. He would nod and continue his leisurely walk. It was the quiet days of fall before we actually became neighborly. One day as he was passing by I asked him to sit and visit a while. That became almost a daily custom during good weather. I kept two chairs in the patio, and when he came along, I would go out and ask him to sit a while. I can see him still. He wore clean, blue overalls and a broad-brimmed black felt hat. His two little dogs would settle in the shade beneath his chair, and, placing the tips of his fingers together, he would usually begin: "Now I'm gonna tell you about the old days . . . ."

Louie was born in Corrales in 1880, son of Noyla and Rita Chavez, in a house across the road and little north of where he lived now. In 1903 and again in 1904 when the big waters hit Corrales, Louie's grandfather's home was washed away, along with many other houses in Corrales. When Louie was fourteen his parents moved into Albuquerque, two doors from the Old Town Society Hall which was on the corner of Rio Grande and Central then. When the seventh child was born, Louie's mother died, and the father and children moved into the old Casa de Armijo, famous now as La Placita Dining Rooms.

Louie grew up in the shadow of San Felipe Church, and it was a strong influence on his life. He helped serve Mass for fourteen years, and he could still recite Mass in Latin like a priest, which was pure magic sitting in the sunshine of my back yard.

I think Louie regretted in some ways not going into the priesthood. When he was twenty-two he fell in love with and married Sixta Martinez, and all thoughts of becoming a priest fled. In those later years when I knew him he spoke lovingly and sometimes longingly of the Church, but as a man who had faced the fact long ago that it was not possible to have everything; he had made his choice, and would do the same thing again.

He remembered serving under nine fathers at San Felipe, but the one he remembered best was Father Quarento (Father Forty) who taught him Latin. Another one, Father de Palma, used to take Louie with him to San Ignacio, a little village on the Herrera Land Grant forty miles west of Albuquerque, where Louie helped conduct Mass. They always went over on Monday, conducted Mass on Tuesday, and returned to Albuquerque on Wednesday. His eyes danced when he told how he and Father de Palma raced their horses on the way.

Sometimes Louie would tell me stories he had heard from others, "about the old days when I wasn't alive," he would say, assuring me it was not an eyewitness account. "Those Navajos are smart people," he would say. "They used to come here and steal things — horses, cows, even women and children. One time there was a little boy with nine sheep. His name was Martinez. Two Navajos came over the *ceja* (brow of the west mesa) and took him and the sheep. Someone saw them, so three Spanish men got on horses and rode after them. They found the boy and his sheep several miles west. The Navajos had left them and escaped. The boy was all right except he was hungry and thirsty."

"Another time there were two women washing clothes out in the yard of their big house. You remember those big black kettles women used to wash in? A whole band of Navajos swooped down and carried off the youngest woman. There must have been twenty or twenty-five Navajos and they rode away fast.

"The alarm was spread through Corrales, and my grandfather, José Chavez, and four others who had good horses went after them. When they got over near the Rio Puerco they saw the Navajos in the valley below. There were only five Spanish men against many Indians, so the Spanish men wanted to make it look like they had a whole army. My grandfather rode back and forth, waving his sombrero and shouting "Vengase! Vengase!" as if he had a big party riding up the hill behind him. Then the five Spaniards charged. They made up a good holler and it sounded like more. The Navajos rode away, leaving the Spanish woman. My grandfather was chosen to bring her home, and the others went on chasing the Navajos. Next day they had not come home, so other men from the village went to see what had happened. In the valley of the Rio Puerco they found the four Spanish men, all dead, but there were signs of a great struggle where the Navajos had ambushed them. A man from Santa Ana came along who told them he had seen the fight. He said the Spaniards fought so hard the sun stood still."

Louie and Sixta died quite a few years ago. Their daughter and her family live in their house, the fifth generation of Chavezes on the same land.

If I should live to be a hundred, and if I should move to the other side of the world, I could still shut my eyes, say "Corrales," and the first picture to come to my mind would be Louie Chavez sitting in my patio, the warm sun on his big black hat, his two little dogs asleep under his chair, the birds singing in the bosque, and Louie, after a long and comfortable silence, touching the tips of his fingers together and saying, "Now I'm gonna tell you how it used to be."

By the middle of April the nights begin to warm up, and it's safe to plant the garden, but it doesn't grow much for two or three weeks, so there's no hurry.

The hummingbirds come between the ninth and fifteenth of the month, almost as punctually as the swallows to Capistrano. We usually put out nectar for them by the twelfth, whether we've seen any or not, and within hours they begin to appear. Those that have been here before make a beeline for the feeder. Newcomers nudge around the artificial red flowers a bit before they find the nectar. Immediately they become territorial, and after drinking, perch on a limb above the feeder and try to chase off other hummers. In a few days they begin their mating dances. The female sits unconcernedly on a limb, drumming her talons in boredom, while the male swings back and forth in an arc or half circle, trying to attract her attention. The arc may be anywhere from two to six feet across, depending on how enthusiastic his passion is. He makes a loud buzzing noise all the while. I guess he manages to get her attention, because we have plenty of hummingbirds.

Orioles and grosbeaks appear in April and spend the summer, but the lazuli buntings and western tanagers just stop briefly on the their way north. For several years I thought the buntings were bluebirds until one year an indigo bunting was with them. I have never seen a bluebird in the bosque, but I have seen them in the foothills of the Sandias, flocks of a hundred or more, swirling like blue mist across the foothills.

When the Russian olive trees first begin to leaf out it looks like a thin grey smoke in the bosque, and cottonwoods begin to form a green umbrella above. The bosque is alive with the sounds of life. Birds dart from tree to tree with grass and straw hanging from their bills. Squirrels run up trees and grab what's left of last season's olives; pheasants strut along the ditch bank making their raucous call, so ill-suited to their gorgeous plumage. Sometimes a road runner comes through the yard, a mouse or lizard dangling from his beak. He cocks his head toward the house, lowers his tail, leans forward almost parallel to the ground, as streamline as an arrow, and hurries on about his business. When running the feathers on top of his head stand straight up. When he stops the head feathers go down and his tail comes up.

In the midst of the fullness of April, when my cup overflows with appreciation for what the Lord hath given, the IRS taketh away. Which bears out the philosophy of my friends from Jemez. They are convinced that when we receive a lot of a good things, some bad thing will follow, good and bad have to balance. One year we had an unusually good crop of piñon nuts up in the mountains, and they sounded their alarm. Sure enough, that was the year crime hit an all-time high.

To ease the pain of thinking about the IRS, I go out and gather wild asparagus, look at the big red tulips like cups of sunshine, listen to the birds, examine the buds.

The last few days of April often turn stormy again, as if winter can't let go. The wind howls and great clouds of dust swirl over the valley, hiding the mountains. Big cumulus clouds fill the sky, dark and ominous on the bottom. It doesn't smell like summer rain, only like dust, but soon thunder crashes and big drops begin to plop down. It frightens the birds to silence, the sky opens and torrents of rain wash down.

Next day the bosque and field are washed clean, and the brilliant morning sunshine brings up a mist from the ground. As I gaze toward the mountains a gaudy cock pheasant emerges like magic from the mist — rosy breast, iridescent green on head and wings, strutting and proud, an absolute marvel of color and self confidence.

Oh, April, you unpredictable, lovely, extravagant month. Every year you renew us, help us forget our cynicism, disappointments, help us forget wars and violence, pain and cruelty. You show us that no matter what insanity man indulges in, the earth is a work of art and a sanctuary.

MAY. Matachines dancers celebrate the fiesta honoring San Ysidro in Corrales.

ↄↄ

MAY

The Richness of May

The bosque is full of life and growth and smells. Sweetest is the scent of the tiny yellow blossom of the Russian olive trees, insignificant alone, but overwhelming when multiplied by the thousands. Their fragrance blesses the bosque with a silky perfume worthy of a queen's chamber. Especially on a warm spring evening the scent hangs in the air, like an element that has a life of its own. Surely on such a moonlit night Oberon, Titania and all their friends are dancing in the bosque.

The bosque has changed in the years we have been here. The olive trees used to be so thick on our property we couldn't see the barbed wire fence along the edge, and it was almost that dense across the ditch in the bosque. There are not nearly so many now, but it must be a natural process because we have never cut a live one. Russian olives reseed themselves easily, grow fast and die young, often taking root near the base of a cottonwood tree. As it grows it competes for sunshine and nourishment, and the bigger tree wins. One year a disease wiped out most of the Russian olive trees, but they are making a comeback.

It may not be so with the cottonwoods; they may be an endangered species, at least along the Rio Grande. Since the river is controlled by so many dams and reservoirs now, there are no annual floods any more, and that is how the cottonwood forests were propagated. Seeds were washed downstream and deposited on flood plains, sand bars and along the bank where they took root. Now that the river no longer floods, we may be enjoying the last of the mighty, gnarled valley cottonwood, so much a part of the Rio Grande Valley since before recorded history began here.

One May morning in 1962, May 21 to be exact, I smelled smoke. By the time I became aware of it, I realized it had been in my subconscious for some time. I walked around the house and yard, sniffing and looking, but found nothing. At noon I took a sandwich out in the patio and sat down to eat. There was a curious reddish cast to the sunlight, and the smell of smoke was stronger. I began to notice tiny bits of ashes falling around me, so I jumped in the car to go see where the fire was. By the time I got to the highway, out from under the canopy of trees, I could see it in the bosque south of us. Smoke and flames were billowing up into the air fifty and a hundred feet.

By this time everyone else had noticed the fire too, and things broke loose. Fire engines began arriving, neighbors dropped whatever they were doing, grabbed a shovel and ran to help. I left the car by the highway, at least it would be safe if the house burned, and ran home to start hosing down the roof. A plumber working at a neighbor's joined me, and we spent the afternoon on the roof.

It had been a dry spring and years of dead leaves and brush lay on the floor of the bosque. The fire was being pushed rapidly north by a stiff breeze. We found out later it had started just north of the bridge, probably from someone's picnic fire the day before which was a Sunday. It had smoldered all night, then sprang to life when the wind began to blow Monday morning. Within an hour the fire was directly across the ditch from our property, roaring so loudly the plumber and I had to shout at each other to be heard. The sun was hidden by smoke, the flames shot high into the air, leaping from top to top, devouring the green cottonwoods as if they were straw. At least a hundred volunteers, mostly just people who lived in Corrales, were on our property, beating out sparks that leaped across the ditch. They had started south of us and kept even with the fire. Trucks from the volunteer fire departments in Corrales, Paradise Hills and Alameda were there, and Harvey Jones with his pumper truck, following the fire north along ditch roads.

Several times I heard someone shout "Fire!" on our property, and immediately people pounced on it with shovels and beat it out. A spark landed on the head of a friend, and burnt a little of her hair before someone saw it.

Suddenly the wind shifted and blew the fire east toward the river, away from our place and other homes near the ditch. All afternoon the wind blew hard, first one way then another, but finally, a while before dark, they were able to get the fire under control with trenches and back fires. Several dozen of us patrolled the ditch banks all night to keep the fire from coming across to the houses on the west side of the bosque. Burning limbs fell all night, crashing in a shower of red sparks, and setting fire to ground brush it has swept above all afternoon. For more than a week hot spots smoldered, but eventually it burnt itself out. No homes were damaged, thanks to the three volunteer fire departments, and the dozens of Corraleseños who ran to help.

But who can count the birds and other small creatures who were killed or dispossessed. The next morning after the fire there were seven quails in our yard — we had never seen them there before. We saw rabbits darting along the ditches, and for days birds flew aimlessly overhead.

After the fire was all out we walked through the burned area from about a mile south to a half mile north of us. The earth was black and bare. Charred snags stuck up like decayed teeth. It took years for the signs of the fire to disappear, in fact, even now we can still find traces of blackened stumps. There have been many fires in the bosque, and we have helped fight our share of them, but never one as bad as the one in 1962. The bosque from Corrales bridge north about six miles is now protected by the Village of Corrales, the Nature Conservancy, and the City of Albuquerque. Vehicular traffic, fires and shooting are banned, so we may not have any more such disastrous fires. People are allowed to walk into the bosque from the north and south ends, but usually people who care enough to walk into a place are not careless enough to go away and leave a fire burning.

The Nature Conservancy, a national organization, raised $27,000 a few years ago to help set aside the Corrales bosque as a wildlife and nature preserve. Besides the fact that the cottonwood trees themselves may be endangered, the bosque provides habitat for dozens of breeding birds, including the redheaded woodpecker (endangered in New Mexico), the wood duck, eastern kingbird and the gray catbird which rarely breeds anywhere else in New Mexico.

Another fire I remember well, and an example of the efficiency of well-wishing friends, happened at the Johnson's. The Judge and Mrs. Johnson were sitting before the fireplace one chilly May evening, waiting for dinner. A great dane, as usual, lay at the Judge's feet. Suddenly the domestic peace was broken by a roar. "Was that an airplane?" asked Mrs. Johnson. "No, it came from above the fireplace." said the Judge, jumping up to investigate. Within seconds smoke was pouring out the vents, and flames began to leak through the dry latilla ceiling.

Mr. and Mrs. Clark, who lived in the guest house, heard the Judge shout and came running. The men climbed to the roof and began working with the garden hose and axes. Mrs. Johnson ran to the phone and called the Sadlers, across the road. Mr. Sadler slammed down the phone and ran out the door, yelling to his wife to call the fire department. "Where's the fire?" she asked as he ran across the yard, leaping fences like a twenty-year-old. He tripped on Johnson's front step, fell and numbed his knee, but continued into the house on all fours, which looked a little strange to the Johnsons.

Mud and water were flowing freely. The fire was between the two ceilings, and like most adobe houses, there was a four inch layer of dirt between the ceilings for insulation.

Mrs. Sadler called fire departments in Corrales, Alameda, Paradise Hills and Albuquerque, but before any of them got there the place was alive with neighbors, whose calm, cool cooperation was a beautiful thing to see: Eleanor Sadler was walking through mud and water dusting the furniture; Mrs. Clark was seen carrying light globes outside; Grace Caplin saw a hose that was leaking a little stream, so she picked it up, climbed a ladder and directed the water down a vent.

After it was all over, someone made coffee and invited everyone to have something to eat. The Judge picked up a piece of chicken he had been ready to eat three hours earlier. "This is the coldest thing in the house," he said.

I miss those days when everything was done by volunteers and neighbors. Nowadays everyone wants a government grant, but people haven't changed much. When there's a crisis, they still drop everything and run to help. Today we have a shiny fire truck, a rescue squad, a few partly-paid people and a well-trained crew of volunteers. We didn't have any kind of fire department until 1953 when the first volunteer group was organized. Jasper Koontz donated a calf to raffle off which, with other fund raisers, brought in enough to build a little cinder block building which was half library and half fire station, and to buy a second or third clunker of a fire truck. Every year for a long time there was a Fireman's Ball to raise money to support the fire department.

The benefit in 1959 was not a ball, but an old fashioned melodrama using local talent. Dory Cornelius wrote it and called it "Corrales Sal." Sis Koontz played the lead, a demure lass whose honor was in constant jeopardy. The can-can girls flounced enthusiastically, showing ruffled panties and black net stockings. Suzie Poole belted old favorites, her beautiful voice bouncing off the adobe walls of Perea Hall like thunder.

Even though our fire department now is more modern and better equipped, we still don't take it or any other facility for granted. We remember what it took to get them started.

One May morning a Wilson's warbler flew against the sliding glass door in the dining room so hard he fell unconscious to the ground. I went out and picked him up, expecting him to have a broken neck. He was only about four inches long from beak to tail, bright yellow with a glossy black skull cap. After a minute or two he opened his eyes and peeked out through the circle of my thumb and forefinger where he was cupped in my hands. He blinked, and I could actually feel his body vibrate with his heart beat. I walked out in the field away from the house, talking baby talk to him. I lifted my top hand which was covering him, expecting him to fly away, but he sat in the cup of the other hand, watching me trustingly. I lifted him off my hand and set him on a willow branch. His feet took hold and he looked fine, but he continued to sit and stare at me. I walked away about ten feet, then walked back, picked him up again. I put him on my forefinger and held him up high. Finally he flew to the fence along the edge of the field, sat there a little while, then flew back and landed on a branch just above my head. I wish I could have stayed longer to see if he would land on my hand again, but just then one of the cats sauntered out to see what was going on, so I picked up the cat and went back to the house.

Never, before or since, has any other bird acted this way, though I've rescued many from various fates. This little warbler must have knocked out all his memory for a few minutes, and when he came to in my hand, must have somehow confused me with his mommy.

All through May we find halves of bird eggshells on the ground, so I know all is right on schedule. The fledglings are almost as big as their parents by the time they leave the nest. One year I saw mother robin teach three hulking youngsters a few of the facts of life. She hopped along pecking at the ground. Two of the young ones caught on right away and followed suit. The third one stood in one place and fluttered his wings, beak wide open, waiting for mommy to put something down his throat. She did several times, but then her patience was exhausted. Next time she just walked up to him and bumped him, breast to breast. The youngster looked astonished, but soon began hunting and pecking for himself.

The mother robin flew up to the bird bath and took a drink. Fledglings followed, first pecking at the water as they had at the ground, then like their mother, raised their heads and let it run down their throats. Satisfied with a good afternoon's work, they flew off together, sat beside each other on a limb, surveying the bosque.

On May 15 Corrales celebrates its patron saint, San Ysidro, with a fiesta. Sometimes the fiesta lasts two days with religious and secular activites. The patron saint of farmers, San Ysidro is probably the best loved and most celebrated saint in New Mexico, other than Our Lady of Guadalupe, the patron saint of all New Mexico and Mexico. Fiesta begins at the 'old church' (second-to-last) with a blessing of the saint, then a procession down the dusty road to the new church on the highway. Matachines dancers and musicians lead the way. Some years there are candlelight processions, Blessing of the Animals, food, arts and crafts booths, games, parades and dances. Particulars vary from year to year according to the parishioners who plan it.

Old-timers say that when they were children the fiesta was bigger than it is today. School was dismissed, women baked for days, houses were re-plastered, rooms were whitewashed, everyone visited everyone else, there were games and refreshments in front of the church, and a dance lasted all night.

Lurlie Silva, up in her eighties now, remembers the Fiesta of San Ysidro as the most important celebration of the year, but she remembers other fiestas too, like the one to celebrate cleaning out the ditches. This was held in early spring before farmers began irrigating. It had its basis in the practical need to clean weeds and the winter's collected debris out of the ditches so the water could run freely. But having a fiesta made it fun for everyone instead of work. Farmers started at the north end of the village and cleaned the *acequia madre* (mother ditch) to the south end of the village. Farmers dropped in and out of the work crew as it passed by their farms; villagers followed along, making an impromptu parade along the dusty village road (it's paved now, but still the only road through Corrales) to meet the ditch cleaners in the bosque at the south end of the village. They brought food and music, and Lurlie's father always furnished a big barrel of homemade red wine. He was the best *vintero* in Corrales, Lurlie said.

Lurlie has lived here all her life, and has watched many things go up and down the road in front of her house. She remembers when she was a little girl seeing herds of sheep, goats, horses or cows on their way to market in Albuquerque. Corrales Road was the old post or stagecoach road that went from Albuquerque to San Ysidro and on up to La Ventana (gone now) and Cuba. A branch went to Jemez Indian Pueblo. She remembers seeing farmers, Indian and Spanish, walking or driving wagons on the road. Itinerant clowns passed by on their way from village to village. They would perform in anyone's yard for a few centavos or a bag of corn or a hot meal. She remembers seeing peddlers, sometimes on foot, sometimes on horseback or riding donkeys. She said they sold *chiquitos*, small baskets, *guallaves*, corn bread made on hot stoves, and *tasagos*, melons dried and cut in strips and made into fancy rolls.

Lurlie's grandmother, a French woman, was the first doctor in Corrales. She came to New Mexico by wagon train across the Santa Fe Trail soon after the Civil War. She had a little adobe hospital near the river which was washed away by flood one year, but she spent many years treating patients all the way from Bernalillo to Isleta. She made her rounds, Mrs. Silva remembers, in a neat black buggy, driving her own team of handsome black horses. Psychology and coffee grounds were tools of her trade as much as the pills she carried in her satchel. In those days most people in New Mexican villages believed in witch-craft, so Dr. Vernier made use of superstition in her treatments. She would have coffee with a patient first, then look in their cup, cluck sym-pathetically, and say, "You have *mala suerte*," (bad luck).

"*Como, como?*" they would say, "how do you know?"

"From the grounds in your cup," she would say, and proceed to treat them, sometimes going so far as to roll up a ball of horsehair and by sleight-of-hand make them think she removed it from their stomach.

Lurlie grew up, married into the Silva Family, and raised a family of her own plus several other children. She used to stand at her front door and watch them walk out to the road to catch the school bus to Bernalillo. There was no school in Corrales.

Lurlie still sits on her front porch and watches people passing by, but they are all in cars now, hurrying to and from work, and too rushed to stop and chat. The traffic is so heavy she no longer dares cross the road.

JUNE. *Houses now fill the orchard where Mr. Griego grew such fine cherries. Cherry picking time was almost like a fiesta.*

⟡

JUNE

Cherry Picking Time

This sweet and fragrant land lies still in the summer heat. The skies are brittle-blue, shining like satin. No clouds, no movement, only the little close sounds that are easy not to hear, like the crack of seeds as grosbeaks and finches feed at their feeder, and the small rustling sound as an oriole swings on the hummingbird feeder. He steals one sip and spills ten.

The *yerba de manza* is full and green, and sometimes people come to dig it up. The roots, when dried, make a tea that tastes worse than sassafras so it must be good for you. It's suppose to cure anything wrong with the tummy except pregnancy. Wild spinach or lambs quarters is up now, and does a lot for a salad.

In June flower gardens begin to look impressive. Roses, pansies, pentunias, lobelia and flax daub the flower beds like an artist's palette. My favorite flower garden is a Flower Garden quilt my mother made. She made quilts all her life; we used them before electric blankets were invented, and when we still used feather mattresses. During the depression she made a few to sell. She was considered a very good quilter because her stitches were small and regular. My brother graduated from Las Cruces high school in 1932 and Mom made a quilt she sold for $25.00, a good price in those days. It brought Don a new suit and shoes for graduation. She used to help the ladies at church make quilts to give to people who needed them, or to sell at church bazaars. Sometimes she had a quilting bee at home, and they often finished a quilt in one day. It would already be "pieced" or sewn together, so on the day of the bee it would be ready to put on the frame which Mom and Dad had put up the day before in the front room. A plain piece of material for the underside would be fastened to the frame first, then the inner lining, usually made of old thin woolen blankets or cotton batting, then the top which was made in some pattern of tiny pieces sewn together by hand. Sometimes it was a hodge-podge of various sizes and shapes, called a "crazy quilt." No good quilter would have considered sewing the pieces together by machine.

At the bee three or four women worked on both sides, quilting around each little piece, and when a row (as far as they could comfortably reach) was finished, they rolled the wooden frame toward the middle, and by the end of the day, both ends would be rolled up until the women were touching hands along the middle of the quilt. I used to love those quilting bees. They made me feel grown up, listening to the easy conversation and laughter of the women, and when I was old enough, it became my job to make lunch for them.

When Mom made a quilt by herself, it sometimes took weeks to finish the quilting, and maybe it had taken a year to piece it together. Mom was particular about piecing it, matching the colors carefully, and when she finished, it was a work of art. Even when we were kids, we admired the quilts, and after Mom no longer needed to make them for warmth or money, she made one as a gift for each of us. Double Wedding Ring, Dresden Plate and Flower Garden were her favorite patterns. Mine is a Flower Garden. Each flower "bed" begins with a hexagon of solid color, surrounded by a circle of hexagons in contrasting solid color, surrounded by a circle of hexagons in a matching print, surrounded by a circle of hexagons of unbleached muslin, making a flower bed about fourteen inches across. These are put together with small green diamond-shaped pieces, so the whole quilt is a colorful garden of flower beds connected by green stepping stones. The only material she bought was the muslin and the green material for the paths. All the rest were scraps of dresses, aprons, shirts or window curtains she had made. There were always scraps of new material left from making anything, and in a year's time she would accumulate a trunk full.

When I put my Flower Garden on the bed it brings back old memories: how Mom looked at the quilting frame, the apron she had on when she took hot bread from the oven on a cold day, the dress she made for my first day of high school in Las Cruces. That was a small lavender print with a lavender yoke connected to the dress with a yellow briar stitch. It was the prettiest school dress I ever had, and eased the uncertainty of being a freshman.

Not many children have a memory lane like my quilt. Even my own children don't. Maybe what children today have is as good or better. They will remember their mother taking them to scouts, soccer games, tennis practice, E.T. and driver's education. Maybe they will remember how their mother worked to help send them to college, and how they all learned to share the work at home because Mom was working and couldn't do it all. I hope these memories are as rich as my flower garden quilt, but I doubt if they are.

June is a hard month for farmers — long, hot hours of irrigating, weeding, pushing things to be ready for market. In Corrales it gets harder every year for farmers to resist the temptation to subdivide and develop. It takes a farmer who really loves to farm, to stay with it today; people like Ernest Alary, Dulcelina Curtis, Ida Gutierrez, the Wagners. Or Miguel Griego.

He's dead now, but for a long time Mr. Griego had a wonderful cherry orchard. He told me once about his orchard. He even remembered the day he bought his first trees, February 20, 1914, when he was just a young man. A nursery salesman from Colorado came through Corrales with a catalogue showing all kinds of growing stock. He told young Miguel about a new cherry tree, a big black sweet cherry grafted onto the root of a malaga, a wild Italian pear tree of unusual hardness. It looked good to Miguel so he ordered thirty of the trees, but his mother, matriarch of the family, did not like the idea of ordering anything from a book without seeing it first.

"No es un arbol," she said, "es un cuadro, no mas." And she closed her mouth, mind and the discussion. Miguel was a good son, and wanted to obey his mother, but he had his own ideas about farming, so he compromised and cut his order to fifteen cherry trees, two pear, and three apple trees. The trees cost .20 each, he told me, and shipping cost another $4.20, making a total of $8.20 for the order of twenty trees. It was remarkable that he could remember such precise details after fifty years, but it proved how important it was to him, and what a big step he was taking to order them in spite of his mother's advice.

When the trees came they were about six feet high and he pruned them back to three feet. It was too early in the year for the ditches to have water in them yet so he borrowed a wagon and tank from a neighbor, J.F. Silva, and hauled water from the river to keep the young trees alive.

Five years later he harvested his first crop, and for over fifty years his cherries continued to produce a fine crop every year. The trees grew to a tremendous size, the largest ones reaching a spread of more than sixty feet with trunks more than twelve feet in circumference. The flavor was exquisite and he always found a ready market for his cherries at local stores. Every year the Griegos had their own Cherry Picking Fiesta with members of his family and friends all pitching in to help. There were music and food and lots of laughter, and the pickers could eat all they wanted.

A few years after his original purchase Mr. Griego tried to get more trees like the first ones, but there were no more to be had. The government had stopped the import of the malaga root. The nursery sent him some trees they claimed were similar to the first one, but they never grew as large or produced such fruit.

Mr. Griego is gone now, and so are his trees. The last one died about the same time he did, in the late seventies. Houses stand where his trees grew.

Farmlands in Corrales used to begin at the bank of the Rio Grande. When ditches washed out, as they often did, farmers could carry buckets of water from the river to irrigate their gardens. The work isn't quite that backbreaking now, with all the machines, and the water controlled by dams and ditches, but the changes have taken away some of the farmland. When drainage ditches and the network of irrigation ditches were built in the early 1930s by the Middle Rio Grande Conservancy District, it reclaimed some land for farming, but took away other land that had been farmed.

The Alary family, for instance, lost about a fourth of their farmland during this time, but overall, there was probably a net gain. Ernest Alary, fourth generation member of this Corrales family, is one of the best known farmers in Corrales Valley. His great-grandparents were part of the influx of French families that came here in the last quarter of the last century in such numbers that Corrales was called The French Village for a time. Louis and Josephine Alary bought land here in 1879, and not long afterward she died of smallpox, but her husband and two sons continued to farm, and Ernest is a son of one of the those sons.

Just to the left of the entrance to the old church is the grave and headstone of Josephine Alary. She was buried in the cemetery on the other side of the highway by the church which was destroyed in the big flood of 1904. Some coffins were washed away and never recovered, and grisly stories are still told of finding bodies in various positions in the caskets, but Josephine Alary's family was able to re-bury her casket in front of the new church which was built on higher ground.

Several early immigrant families came to Corrales from Italy, such as the Salces. Angelo Salce left Venice in the early 1880s when he was a boy, and came to New Mexico by way of Mexico. He first bought a farm in the north valley, and moved to Corrales about ten years later. Like most old-world men, he sent back to Italy for a bride, and they had five children born here. Maria, the wife and mother, died in the flu epidemic in 1918, and the children grew up working on the farm. Two daughters, Ida Gutierrez and Dulcelina Curtis, still are well-known farmers in Corrales.

It is not easy nowadays, with high labor costs, government paper work, competition and the constant pressure to sell their land for real estate development, but there is something about putting a seed in the ground, watering it and watching it grow, that keeps farming from being a mere job.

Farmers may become an endangered species. If they die, a part of America will die with them. Maybe their legacy will be carried on by backyard gardeners. No one can blame a farmer for giving up the physically wearing, uncertain and low-paying job of farming in favor of becoming wealthy just by selling his land.

Maybe San Ysidro has had a hand in keeping farmers on the farm. He is revered more than any other saint in Corrales. The church is named for him, a fiesta is held in his honor every May, and lots of people have a San Ysidro santo hanging in their homes. My santo of San Ysidro Labrador (St. Isidore the Farmer) was made by Jorge Sanchez when he lived in Truchas. In his walking along the steep hillsides of Truchas one day he found an old hand-wrought metal hoe. Its rough, uneven, heavy head was the kind a farmer in a small village in New Mexico would have forged by hand during colonial times before manufactured goods were brought across the Santa Fe Trail. Iron was scarce and the hoe would have been handed down to several generations. When Sanchez found it, he knew it was perfect to use for a santo of San Ysidro.

All the farmers loved San Ysidro. He was a man of the soil, like them, a paisano, a hard worker. He knew what it took to eke out a living in the high, narrow valleys of New Mexico, or even along the wide Rio Grande.

In my santo, San Ysidro stands on one side, hands folded in prayer, twice as big as any other character in the picture. He is dressed in what farmers in colonial times wore, a medium length coat and breeches tucked into knee-high boots or leggings, a flat-crowned wide-brimmed hat with a jaunty red feather in it. The angel is holding the reins of an ox team pulling a homemade wooden plow. Plowed fields are in the foreground, and across the bottom is written: "*Recuerde Vd. al Sr. Dios*" (Remember the Lord God.)

Usually San Ysidro is depicted holding the plow with the angel walking beside him, blessing him because he was such a devout man, one who prayed even as he worked. The story Sanchez told me for my santo is a little different, and I prefer it:

Ysidro was a good farmer and loved the Lord God but never took time away from his fields to pray, much less to rest all day Sunday. In the small mountain villages of the north, like Truchas, the land they could farm was small, and the seasons short. He had to work the land hard to feed his family so he let his wife do the praying for him. One year the angel appeared to him and said. "Ysidro, if you do not take the time to pray once in a while, at least on Sunday, I will send a plague of locusts to destroy your crops."

Ysidro did not take time away from his work, so sure enough, the angel sent a plague of locusts that ate almost every stalk of corn. Ysidro worked harder than ever, planting new crops, but the harvest was poor.

The next summer the angel returned and again asked him to remember the Lord God in prayer, or she would send a drought to destroy the crops. All summer Ysidro watched the skies, and there were many signs, but little rain. In order to keep a few things alive he had to dig more ditches and carry hundreds of goatskin bags of water, just so his children would not starve. He worked harder and longer than ever and had no time to pray.

The third year the angel came back and said she would give him one more chance, but if he disobeyed her, she would send floods to wash away everthing he owned.

The drought of the previous year was over. The rains fell and his corn was full and heavy. He worked all the daylight hours, as long as there was light to see his hoe ahead of him. But alas, a week before he was to harvest his crops, the heavens opened up, a cloudburst fell, washing away every single stalk. Heartsick but determined, he began planting again as soon as the water was gone, and a few days later the angel, an old acquaintance by now, appeared for the last time.

"Ysidro," she said philosophically, "I plow, you pray." And this is why in my santo the angel holds the reins of the ox team, and why San Ysidro is the patron saint of farmers.

Remembering San Ysidro and his flood, reminds me of the trials and tribulations we had with water the first summer we moved to Corrales. Anyone moving to the country should know about pumps. Out here water is more than just turning a tap. Our pump didn't work very well, having been idle for over a year, so I got in touch with a Mr. Tinker, who, the neighbors said, had driven the well and installed the pump originally. I should have suspected something, a pump man named "tinker"? Right away he told me he was a "libator," but only because it was necessary for his heart condition.

The day he came was a lovely summer day which he enjoyed most of from the comfort of a lawn chair. Several times he made trips to the nearest hardware store for parts. He took the pump apart, and eventually got it back together again, and it worked. Unfortunately, when I turned on the water inside the house, a good-sized leak shot up from the pipe where it came from the well. Mr. Tinker had had enough for one day, and so had I, so I drew enough buckets to last through the night, he turned off the water at the well and promised to return the next day.

He brought a friend to help fix the pipe. Every time the pump came on, water sprayed from the leak like blood from a cut artery. Mr. Tinker and friend pulled two chairs near the problem area, the better to contemplate the possibilities and libate. All day it was dig and drink, drink and dig. By mid-afternoon they had diagnosed the problem. It was not the pump, nor was it the leak, they said, but we had a spring somewhere down there. They assured me they had it fixed, but when I turned on the water a fountain come up someplace else. I was grateful when evening came, I paid them and they left, promising to return.

Next morning I called another pump man from the yellow pages who replaced the pipe and put in a new pump. Late in the day Mr. Tinker did, indeed, return, so libated he could hardly walk. When he looked in the pumphouse and saw the new pump he was furious. He demanded his violin back which he had brought to have my husband appraise, and left. I never saw or heard of him again.

In a reasonable length of time we had trouble with the new pump. One day it just wouldn't go on, so I called a Mr. Thistlewaite who had been recommended as a good pump repair man. We had a long and fruitful association with Mr. Thistlewaite. He should have had a chair at the University of Heidelburg. He was pumphouse philospher. His voice was melodious and impressive, and he enjoyed the sound of it as much as I did. He could discourse with great solemnity and beauty on comparative religion, literature, geology, entymology, medicine and French cooking. But he was also a good pump man.

Like one time when the pump wouldn't come on. After checking the fuses and switch I called him. "Just go hit it with the handle of a screwdriver," he said. I did, and it worked. His telephonic diagnosis was cobwebs. A well house, he said, is a favorite hangout for black widows and other kinds of spiders and insects. Sometimes a miniscule bit of web or dust gets into some parts of the motor or controls, and a sharp rap is all it takes to jar it loose. I really do miss Mr. Thistlewaite.

You get water into a house, you also have to get it out, and that's where septic tanks, grease traps and drain fields come in. It seemed simple enough. Half the house emptied into a septic tank on one side of the house, and half into one of the other. Living close to the river we found the water table was only three or four feet below the surface so our septic tanks had to be pumped out at least once a year, usually in the spring when the water table was highest. I couldn't pump out a septic tank, but I did learn to clean out a grease trap which was just an old drum outside the kitchen wall which was meant to trap the grease before it got into the septic tank. It contained nothing but water from the kitchen sink, so it didn't bother me at all to dig down, remove the lid, and dip out a few buckets full of greasy water. The fun was the expression on people's faces when I would casually mention at a party that I had dug up the grease trap that afternoon.

A few years ago some environmental health agency in the county passed, or caused to be passed an ordinance outlawing ordinary septic tanks, and requiring people to put in a sewage system that supposedly disposes of the waste forever by means of motors and fans and other mechanical devices. Our neighbors put one in and not only did it cost thousands of dollars, take two weeks to install, dig up an area half the size of a football field, but it has never worked. Hardly a month goes by that they don't have a repair man out to see about it. The warranty has long since run out, and a service call costs as much as a week's groceries.

We have really appreciated our septic tank since then. When we knew how the county was leaning, we hurried and had a new septic tank put in with new drain fields extending in all directions like legs of a spider. We baby it as if it were a Mercedes Benz. Twice a year we put a bottle of stuff in it to help the bacteria dispose of the sludge. We have it pumped out faithfully, and if it slows down when the water table is high in the spring, we hold back on baths and laundry.

*   *   *   *   *   *

The second most important fiesta we have all year is in June. This fiesta built one of the finest small libraries in the country, and continues to help operate it. Until 1957 there was no library in Corrales, not even at the school. Beginning that year the community held bake sales, book sales, card marathons, solicitations and balls to raise money for a library.

We built a little cinder block building next to the school which housed the fire truck on one side and the library on the other. Which made it convenient if you were a volunteer librarian and a volunteer fireman. From 1957 to 1971 the library was staffed entirely by volunteers and supported by annual Adobe Casa Tours. After the village was incorporated in 1971, the library was included in its budget but the community still raised money to help support it and by then the old building was far too small.

So a committee was formed. When Corrales forms a committee, just get out of the way. The Friends of Corrales Library applied for a grant, and when told no money was available for building libraries, they just went out and raised the money. Jerry Tors, an architect, donated his time to draw plans, and several others under the co-chairmanship of Laura Stokes and Nancy Pierce took it on as a full time project. Ground was scheduled to be broken on April 1, 1978. This was not to be a ceremonial groundbreaking with gold shovels and politicians. The ground knew it had been broken. They got seventy-seven good men, women and children with their own hard hats and shovels to dig five feet each of foundation trench. That's the way it went all summer. Troops turned out every Saturday to do whatever he/she did best: plumbers plumbed, electricians wired, judges toted, matrons fetched, doctors mixed mud, musicians laid adobes, teenagers painted. People who weren't so talented gave money. A committee went to the mountains to cut pine trees for vigas; another committee peeled them, and strong backs hoisted them up on the walls. A "topping out" party was held in October, and during the winter work continued on the interior. Brick floors were laid, plumbing and wiring finished, walls painted, shelves built, a decorative fountain built in the atrium, and Pete Smith carved a front desk with separate panels of well known Corrales people: Manuel Martinez, Randolph Armijo, Guadalupe Gutierrez, Trinidad Perea, Filipe Montoya, Clifford Pedroncelli, Horacio Martinez and Dulce Curtis. Eighteen clerestory windows were donated as memorials and several people donated art work. Erickson's Greenhouse landscaped the lobby and atrium.

Kids in the community not only helped build the library, but moved all the books in what was touted as the Great Book Parade. In single file they marched from the school through the old library where they were given an armload of books, down the highway with police stopping traffic, to the new library where they were directed to the proper shelf to put the books. On their way out the door they were given ice cream cones to eat on the way back to the old library for another load.

The Grand Opening was October 7, 1979, eighteen months from the groundbreaking. The 2700 square foot adobe building had required a cash outlay of around $15,000 (raised by contributions), and countless hours of volunteer labor. On today's market it would be worth ten or fifteen times that much.

Every year the Friends of Corrales Library have a Library Fiesta in June. There are games, food, dancing, flea markets, fortune—telling, and Frank Larrabee, a Corrales musician, strong-arms sympathetic musicians to help, and money is raised for the library. By 1982 they had enough put aside to add another room almost as big as the original building. During construction a big sign on La Entrada Road said, "This building is being built through the efforts of interested citizens. Your tax dollars are NOT at work." The new addition is named the Frank Larrabee Room.

JULY. "Old" San Ysidro Church, being restored by the Historical Society, is a good example of a small New Mexican village church.

JULY

When Cicadas Sing

The deep, dark greenness of summer is here, as soft and dark as green velvet. Birds are noisy morning and evening, but in the heat of mid-day they hush. The harsh, loud buzzing of the cicadas is so constant it melds into the subconscious, and we are only aware of it when it stops.

No breeze stirs the leaves. Cottonwood trunks rise slim and crooked, reaching high toward the sunshine above the green canopy. The grey-green of the olive trees below the cottonwoods invites a startled second glance, to be sure they are not smoke. The ground is covered with a thick growth of *yerba de manza*, smelling strong and medicinal when stepped on.

I shrink myself to coolness, sitting quietly in the shade, imagining my body getting smaller inside my clothes, not touching them, and feeling coolness. In the midst of this summer somnolence in the solid, deep shade of the bosque is the time to let the mind flow freely, joining the thread of life in this ancient landscape. Man, bird and beast have followed the Rio Grande forever.

I can feel the presence of the Anasazi, their small brown bodies going quietly through the trees, alert for a bird or rabbit to shoot with their bow and arrow. They may sit in the shade and rest a while, listening to the same sounds I do. Their villages are scattered along the valley, a family or clan living in each one, content with the small crops of corn and squash they raise, the wild grains and fruits they gather, and the game they kill. Theirs was not an affluent society, they had no surpluses, but it was a balanced one and adequate. It was probably the most serene society that ever existed here.

I can feel the presence of the Spanish soldiers, padres and settlers. Those on horseback rattled and clanked with the completely new sound of metal. Ox carts made with wheels cut from trees, held together by wooden axles with little or no grease, made such a screech they must have shocked the birds to stunned silence. The women and children in the parties, when there were women and children, must have loved the relief of the trees after the dreadful trek across Jornada del Muerto.

I can feel the presence of the traders who went down the Chihuahua Trail to Mexico. They, too, followed the river, grateful for the coolness of the trees, the firewood, the rest. They shouted and cursed their mules and oxen, herded their sheep along the trail. They raised great clouds of dust, but like the others before them, they were grateful for the gentleness of the trees near the river, and thought of home and family as they rested with their back against a big cottonwood.

But nothing stays totally quiet for very long in the bosque, and a fat bumblebee brings me back to the present. He crawls into a hollyhock blossom, so coated with pollen he can hardly fly, but he makes a loud, clumsy effort.

A half dozen orioles fly down to the yard, some lighting on the rim of the birdbath, crowding out a sparrow and a robin that were already there. Some splash in the water, others drink. One lands on a stem of a full-blown red rose. As the stem curves over, he manages to hold on with his feet, upside down, and one by one, he pecks out every single petal and lets it fall to the ground. Hanging on the hummingbird feeder upside down, drinking the juice, is no trick at all for them. Black-headed grosbeaks are our most prolific summer resident. Sometimes a dozen are on the feeder at the same time. With them is often a blue grosbeak, dark and sleek. The blues probably nest nearer the ditch, but the blackheads nest in the trees near the house, and their song is glorious. They are not as agile or such clowns as the orioles, but every year a few learn to drink from the hummingbird feeders by staying on the wing underneath it, not by hanging down from above like the orioles.

Sometime in July the peace of a quiet afternoon is shattered by a rufous hummingbird. For anything so small, they are pure loud, raucous, combative, greedy energy, dive-bombing any other bird or bee that approaches the feeder. He is a bright coppery-red dart of pure pugnaciousness. He doesn't need all the juice, he just likes to fight.

It used to bother me to see the rufous hummers come in every July and drive away the docile little black chins that had entertained us since April, had raised their families, had performed their mating flight countless times. How dare this orange intruder who has spent the summer in the mountains, come roaring in like a Hells Angel, in the midst of our summer reverie, and tell us that summer is almost over? But that is exactly what he is saying, and he is driven by a force he cannot resist. He is a signal to the other birds to start thinking about going south. In the midst of the cocoon-like laziness of July comes this little monster, saying summer is over. It may stay hot a few more weeks, but the rufous and I know summer's days are numbered.

One still July afternoon I looked out the window and saw a man walking through the trees toward the ditch. He was small, had long, dark hair, carried a cane, limped slightly, and was accompanied by a big black dog. I went out and intercepted him before he reached the ditch. This is, after all, "Our Property" and I have a right to know who walks on it. He told me he was a Vietnam veteran who had been shot in the leg in Vietnam. He had been living in Rio Rancho in a rented house with his wife and two children. When his veteran's check had been late they had been evicted, so they were camping in the bosque so they could stay close to the post office in Rio Rancho until his check came. He walked through our yard, simply because it was between him and the post office. This meant wading through the ditch, climbing through several barbed wire fences, cutting across yard and fields, and getting barked at by any number of dogs on his way to the top of the mesa and the post office. His silent efficiency impressed me, and I wondered how many battlefields he had walked through, quietly and efficiently.

I offered him iced tea and sandwich, which he refused, climbed through the fence, waded the ditch and disappeared into the bosque. I thought about him all night, and next day set out to find them, knowing I could find help for them, but they were gone. I found their camp, where they had buried their garbage, where they had dug a pit toilet, where they had spread their blankets, where they had cooked over an open fire. The campsite was neat and clean, but a feeling of sadness hung in the air, or maybe I imagined it. He had faced far worse things before, I know. In our time and society it seems sad and desperate to have to live in the bosque without shelter, but maybe his children will remember it as the time they went camping. Maybe he and his wife felt a kinship with the thousands of soldiers, explorers, priests, Spanish colonists, traders and hunters who had followed the Rio Grande for centuries, camping as they went, all seasons of the year, living off the land. Maybe the Vietnam vet felt less like an alien in the bosque than in a rented house on a paved street.

Corrales Adobe Theater was a cherished summertime institution in Corrales for almost thirty years. After Albuquerque Little Theater, which began in the 1930s, Corrales Adobe Theater is the oldest community theater in the area. It started as an idea in 1958 when a group of Corrales citizens decided Corrales needed a little uptown class. They discussed it for a year or two, and in 1959-60 a young director named Doug Koss called on people to see what kind of support a community theater would have if he started one. He found enthusiasm from people like Jean and Bill Carstens and many others, so the theater became a reality. It wasn't always in the old church where most people remember it. It has been in a coffin factory, an old grocery store, a saloon, a restaurant and an apple orchard.

In 1962 when the "new" church was built in Corrales, the old one was de-sanctified and made available to use for other purposes. Corrales Adobe Theatre used it every summer from 1962 through 1987, in spite of falling plaster, poor plumbing, ghosts and other impediments. It wasn't always easy, but it was always fun to have good summer theater in an old church. Adobe gets tired and has a tendency to want to melt back into the earth if left alone. It attracts bugs, worms and bats; you can't dig up the floor because someone's ancestors are buried there; electrical wires don't cling to mud plastered walls; rain pounding on the tin roof often drowned out the actors. But through it all the theater supporters remained loyal, and kept patching up the old building so it would do for another summer of plays.

In 1973 the church got it first real boost toward preservation. Corrales Historical Society was raising money to buy the building from the Diocese, and the first big check came from a Hollywood film company who filmed part of the TV series *Nakia* there.

It was a dramatic scene where it was supposed to look as if the church were being burned down by political activists. Crews had worked for days to get it ready, and when the night came to do the filming, big flames shot out the windows and crawled along the roof. The flames were real, but they were coming out of pipes and controlled so no harm was done. Fire trucks, ambulances and police stood by in case anything went wrong, but nothing did. Robert Blake, the star, and the other cast and crew members worked swiftly and expertly to make the first take perfect - they couldn't do that one twice. Just as they were finishing the shooting, a Corrales girl came rushing to the scene, found the director, started beating him on the chest and screaming, "You can't burn that church - my parents were baptised there."

Next day the film company cleaned up the mess, replastered where the smoke had blackened it, removed the false timbers, and gave the Historical Society a check for a thousand dollars. The Society bought the church, had the building declared a historic landmark, and turned it over to the Village of Corrales. The Historical Society is presently in charge of a major restoration project, and the theatre group will have to find new quarters next summer, but in view of their history, no one doubts the theater will survive. Meantime the old church has once more taken on the appearance of a small village mission church.

Old San Ysidro has seen a lot of activity during its more than a century of use, but probably nothing was more exciting than its night of stardom on film. No one knows exactly when the church was built, but Alan Minge, a most respected Corrales historian, believes it was between 1868 and 1875. A disastrous flood in 1868 washed away an earlier church east of the highway which was replaced by this one on higher ground about a half mile to the west. The present church is on the highway directly east of the old one. All three have been named San Ysidro, to honor the patron saint of Corrales. Several Corrales patriarchs have been buried in front of and inside the old church. One time Lurlie Silva was at old San Ysidro watching some youngsters having a dancing lesson. "You are dancing on my grandmother's grave," she told them, "but she wouldn't mind."

There may have been two small churches built in Corrales in the 1700s. Upper Corrales had one called Santa Rosalia, a mission from the church at Sandia Indian Pueblo across the river. Lower Corrales was under the jurisdiction of San Felipe in Albuquerque, but it is not certain that a church was built there. Most large homes or haciendas had private chapels or oratorios.

Even with all the changes in Corrales, roots are deep, and San Ysidro is honored as the patron saint with a fiesta in the spring. Reverence for tradition and reverence for the earth still exist.

AUGUST. A Corrales chili field.

𝒥𝒞

AUGUST

When Muddy Waters Roll

What the local weathermen refer to as the "monsoon" season begins in August. These thundershowers can be dramatic and exciting, and can drop the temperature fifteen or twenty degrees in a few minutes, but they can also do a lot of damage with flash floods.

Corrales is vulnerable to flash flooding because it lies in the valley between the river and the high mesas on the west side, and the Jemez Mountains to the northwest. Albuquerque used to have flash floods every summer from the Sandias until the huge diversion channels were built.

Important dates in Corrales are often remembered in relation to a flood, like the big floods of 1868 and 1874 that washed away the church and cemetery, and the one in 1904 that caused the name of Corrales to be changed. The last big flood was about ten years ago when fifteen or twenty houses were damaged in the north end of the village. It happened on a beautiful August afternoon. Skies were velvety blue, clouds puffy and white except toward the northwest where by mid-afternoon the sky began to turn purple-black, like a Betty Sabo painting. It didn't rain a drop here, but a cloudburst struck about fifteen miles north in the foothills of the Jemez Mountains, and within thirty minutes a wall of water twelve feet high came. It passed through the Rio Rancho industrial area, washing out the bridge on Hwy. 528 as if it were paper. People working in several plants there said they heard the deafening roar of the water, though most of them didn't see it. When the wall of water hit the high ditch west of Corrales, it was carried only a few hundred yards south before ditch banks broke, spilling muddy water down toward houses and farms that lay between the ditch and the river.

Just like in the old days, neighbors turned out to help — shoveling mud, pumping water, sweeping goo, filling sandbags, and serving coffee and sandwiches. The Red Cross took over a little later, but neighbors continued to help.

Lurlie Silva told me about the big flood of 1904 which she says she remembers, or at least remembers hearing her family talk about. She says the adobe houses "melted like sugar," because in those days no one used hard plaster. (It still happens to adobe walls inside the hard plaster.) Men were working in the fields and saw and heard the water coming down Los Montoyas Arroyo, but were able to divert the water down other ditches, sacrificing one or two large fields which acted like holding basins. All the women and children, Lurlie says, were sent to the top of the ceja to camp out until the threat was over and the mud dried up a little. Children played, women cooked, and men patrolled the ditches for about three weeks, she remembers, reinforcing weak spots and building new dikes. Those whose fields were sacrificed accepted it as a hard fact of life, knowing their more fortunate neighbors would share with them. All, that is, except Mr. Alejandro Sandoval.

"Mr. Alejandro Sandoval was the rich man of Corrales and Bernalillo," said Mrs. Silva. "He owned everything and always took his irrigation water first. But he treated his workmen like coyotes, and lots of people didn't like him. That time after the flood in 1904 he came riding down the ditchbank in his fancy buggy from his fancy home in Bernalillo, and demanded that the workmen open the ditch and drain his property, even if it meant the water would run onto someone else's field.

"The men refused to obey him, and stood their ground. He turned red in the face and waved his whip in the air. His horses got scared and jumped, and turned the buggy over, spilling Mr. Alejandro Sandoval right into the ditch. He looked just like a big red, wet turkey, and none of the men offered to help him out of the ditch."

But Mr. Sandoval got even. Some weeks later he came to see the farmers in Corrales, and asked them to sign a paper so they would get government money to pay for the flood. At that time most of the farmers couldn't read English, so they took his word and signed the paper. It was a petition to change the name of the village from Corrales to Sandoval.

It remained Sandoval for almost seventy years, officially, at least. No one minded very much, because they thought it was so funny. The post office was changed to Sandoval, mail had to be addressed to Sandoval, the school was called Sandoval, state maps showed the village as Sandoval, but the people went right on calling it Corrales, just the same as always. Finally, someone who makes such decisions changed everything back to Corrales.

In the old days, maybe even today, people prayed to San Ysidro when the rains fell hard and flood threatened. One favorite little prayer was "San Ysidro Labrador, *quita el agua y pon el sol.*" (Saint Isadore the Farmer, take away the rain and let the sun shine.) Another was to Santa Barbara for protection during thunder and lightning storms: "Santa Barbara Doncella, *libranos de rayo y la centella.*" (Santa Barbara, maiden fair, deliver us from the thunderbolt and the lightning.) Santa Barbara is usually depicted with a thundercloud and a bolt of lightning.

In spite of, or partly because of the thundershowers, August is one of the best times of year. The sun has a quiet benevolence, not as benign as September, but not as intense as June or July. The pace slackens. The enthusiasm of early summer is spent. Vacations are almost over; children are getting bored, mothers are wishing school would start. Garden vegetables are producing heavily, and it's just a matter of weeding once in a while, and watering if it doesn't rain. There's nothing new to plant, no pruning, no tender nurturing. Fruit stands up the road are filled with tomatoes, corn, peaches, plums, and, best of all, chili.

Oh! Those lovely green, fat pods of sublime addiction. Hatch . . . Chimayo . . . Corrales . . . whose chili is best? What a wonderful problem to be faced with. Each village has its supporters. Where once choices were limited to "hot" and "mild", now we have "torrid", "hot", "medium hot", "mild", "so-so" and "sissy," or adaptations thereof, in a half dozen varieties like "Sandia," "Big Jim", or "Little Jim." Green chili is good in casseroles, sauce, dips, with any meat, eggs, in any sandwich. We even make chili jelly and chili bread. Texans can have that reddish-brown concoction they call "chile" (Kathy Andreson says it look like something that was mugged in the park) but give us our green chili.

Part of the pleasure of chili is going to one of the outdoor stands and buying it. Nowadays we get it roasted in a big wire rotisserie that does it while we stand there smelling it, glassy-eyed and drooling. We used to roast it at home, usually over an outdoor barbecue grill. It took a long time, turning each pod until it was evenly roasted, putting it in layers in hot towels to steam the skins. It was a long, tedious job, but we made it a social event by working on it with a neighbor.

The smell of roasting chili wafts a long ways, and has been known to draw people right off the streets. One year a friend and I were sitting in the shade of a cottonwood tree, leisurely turning chili pods, when another friend picked up the scent and dropped by. I was peeling and packaging some that was already roasted and steamed, and was having a hard time getting all the black, shiny skin off. "You don't have to do that," my neighbor said "My grandmother always told me that you had to leave a little of the black skin on, or it won't taste right." That's the kind of wisdom I like. Since it's almost impossible to get all the black skin off, why not believe it makes it taste better to leave a little on? If you can't lick 'em, join 'em!

August has it share of grasshoppers, and if there are loose guinea hens in the neighborhood, we encourage them to come over by tossing grain in the driveway. By August the young ones are half-grown and can eat a lot of grasshoppers. One year we had a regular pair which we called Pat and Mike, not having the slightest notion which was which, what sex, or where they came from. By mid-August they had a family of seven chicks with them, so round and fat they looked like cartoons as they ran to keep up with their parents. Another adult began coming with them, which we called Uncle Hoppy, though he might have been Aunt Hoppy, because he had just one leg. He was the chick-sitter. He clucked and called them just like their parents did when he found a tasty bug or worm to share. He got along fine with just one leg, hopping as fast as the others walked. He stood tilted on one leg, balancing his weight. Eventually Uncle Hoppy diappeared, and we found him later in the field, a victim of someone's dog. Through the fall and winter the chicks disappeared, one at a time, and the parents too.

We haven't been too successful with grasshopper-eaters. Someone gave us a pair of geese which are supposed to be just as good as guinea hens to eat bugs. We named them Lucy and Hissy, and made a pen in the shade in the front yard where they could see us come and go. Since they were town geese, we thought they would appreciate the thought. They not only appreciated it, they were addicted to people, and never really adjusted to country living. After three days in the pen we turned them loose, herded them toward the garden and pointed out that there were millions of grasshoppers there. They raced us back to the front door, sat in front of the picture window, pecked at the glass, talked to their reflections, and left a lot of dropping on the bricks.

We moved their pen out next to the garden, even bought them a wading pool, but their favorite place was always at the front door and window. We eventually gave them to someone who wanted some geese.

It isn't just the domestic animals we enjoy watching but the wild ones that come over from the bosque. We see muskrats and beavers along the ditches, rabbits and coyotes in the bosque, occasionally in the yard, and I remember one moonlight August night I went for a walk. Coming back toward the house, silhouetted by the front porch light, I saw a family of five skunks, a mother and four little ones. In single file they marched out of the woods across the driveway, with the confidence demonstrated only by a skunk. I stood still, but they saw me and circled like a wagon train, noses to center, tails straight up around the outside of the circle, ready to take aim and fire in any direction if mama gave the word. I didn't move a muscle until they decided all was well and marched on across the driveway into the bosque.

I often saw the skunks that fall, but it was usually early morning, when they were turning over leaves looking for grubs.

SEPTEMBER. *Afternoon thunderheads build up over the Sandias.*

꩜

SEPTEMBER

The Time of Bittersweet Contemplation

The heat and fuss of summer are over. Indian summer flows like a golden stream into September. One day a yellow leaf flutters to the ground, the next there are more. A whole yellow spot appears here and there in the bosque. The deep, dark green of summer that was so rich with life a few weeks ago is ragged now, color and life draining slowly from trees, garden, weeds and grass. Another cycle has passed. Birth, youth, fullness of summer, then death. And then the long cold wait for it to start over again.

Fall is a rare golden time, precious because the days are fleeting and short, a reminder that life is full one day, gone the next. The earth does not belong to us. We share it for a while, then go on and make room for someone else.

September days are still warm, but nights have the bite of fall. It's time to get out the electric blanket. We no longer fuss with the garden, we harvest a squash or two and leave the rest to the grasshoppers.

Almost as if on signal the doves disappear, conditioned probably, by dove season which begins September first. Hunters used to wake us at daylight on the first day of dove season, and many a bullet has whistled through the trees and landed in our yard. Since the Village of Corrales annexed the bosque and prohibited firearms, we seldom hear a dove hunter any more, but the doves got into the habit of leaving the first of September anyway.

In September the Sandias take on an intensity they don't have in summer. They turn magenta in the late afternoon sun, and clouds above them look like balls of flame. September clouds carry a great deal of water still, and heavy thunder showers usually continue through the month. At sunset the mountains are deep red; magenta turns to purple, and swaths of dull reddish-blue streak up the canyons on the west side. In a few minutes they are dull and dark, their brilliance brief and fleeting.

September is an ideal time to hike in the Sandias. Trails aren't so crowded, and the weather is pleasant on either the forested east side, or the open, rocky west side. The first time I hiked to the crest on La Luz Trail was a glorious mid-September day. The first part of the trail is open switchbacks, snaking up the sunny slopes, offering a good view over the mesa and valley. After the trail crosses the first canyon the growth is heavier, trees are taller, stream beds have a trickle of water, and pussy willows and deciduous trees line the banks. Along the upper half of the trail it passes rock gardens of shade-loving plants, clumps of aspen trees, thickets of wild raspberry bushes, moss in cool damp places, columbine nodding gracefully on slender stems. Meadow and hillsides are scattered with blue, purple, red and yellow flowers whose names I can never remember. The last mile or two goes up the steep sides of the limestone strata that was deposited by a great inland sea about 250 million years ago.

I remember the exhilaration that first time I topped the last part of the trail and reached the crest. Tired but exhilarated, I sat down to contemplate my land - mountains and mesas receding into the hazy distance to the west; a silver streak snaking through the valley where the sun glints off the Rio Grande. And there - right there next to that big open field where the bosque is the thickest and the river makes a bend around it - is our house. You can't see it, but it's there.

September has a special quietness. The children are in school, things move in slow motion. Summer birds are almost all gone and winter birds haven't come yet. It is a time to think.

My mother's birthday was September 21, and thoughts of her always come along with the other happy/sad/lonely/accepting September musings. Born into a large family in Arkansas, her father died of measles when she was eight years old. In 1888, her mother brought the four youngest children to Texas to live near the oldest son who was a farmer and school teacher, later in the Texas and New Mexico Legislatures. Ruins of their two log cabins, stone chimneys still standing, are preserved on the land a cousin owns today. Mom taught school when she grew up, like most nice girls did then, until she married my father and moved to New Mexico. With three other young couples they homesteaded land in northeastern New Mexico.

They were "boxcar immigrants." The men came in the fall of 1912, filled on claims and went back to Texas to get ready to move. In March they loaded their horses, milk cows, plows and household goods into a boxcar they had all rented together. Men and older boys rode in the boxcar to take care of the stock, and women, girls and younger children rode in the passenger cars.

The day they got off the train in Des Moines was during the Blizzard of 1913, still remembered as the worst on record. They all found rooms at a hotel where the families lived until the men could get out to their claims and build small frame houses.

None of them expected a homesteader's life to be easy, and it wasn't. But my mother always said those were the very best years of their lives, with the thrill of plowing virgin ground and planting wheat and rye that grew belly high to the horses, raising cabbage, beets and carrots in the garden, and storing them all winter in the cold dug-out cellars under the house. Mom could kill a rattlesnake with a hoe, cook and sew everything her family needed, harness a team and drive a buggy, deliver a baby, or deliver a sermon on Sunday, but she never learned to drive a car or shoot a gun. She wrecked one Model T trying to learn to drive it, and abhorred guns, so she gave up on them. I was not born until after they moved away from the homestead but forever after I noticed how she glowed when she talked about those years, and I felt I missed something important. The boxcar immigrants were the last of the pioneers, and would have gotten along just as well in an ox cart or covered wagon.

The rich and fertile volcanic plains country of northeastern New Mexico should never have been plowed. Dry-land farming was too risky, and all the land plowed by homesteaders like my parents was eventually sold to cattle ranchers and it became part of the dust bowl in the thirties. The scars still show. But the homesteaders didn't know what they were helping to create. And it was these ordinary people — farmers, truck drivers, school teachers, preachers, grocers who settled the west, not the gamblers, outlaws and dance hall girls. The Homestead Act brought them west. They stayed to make it home.

My mother died at age ninety in California, and until three weeks before she died, she had never been in a hospital except to visit a sick friend. The last year of her life she suffered with phlebitis, but she never missed a single day of getting dressed and working around her home. The last few months before her ninetieth birthdays she kept telling the doctor he had to keep her in good shape for her birthday, which he did. That day she cooked dinner for a dozen relatives, and enjoyed every minute of it. I wasn't able to go to her birthday celebration, and the next time she saw her doctor she told him there was one more thing he had to do.

"Another birthday?" he asked.

"No, just until my youngest daughter gets out here to see me." I went out six weeks later, arriving on a Friday afternoon. After a good dinner which she had partly cooked and completely supervised, she started telling me about her funeral plans. Even though I knew what an organized person she was, I was taken back at first, but then I realized that was exactly why she had wanted me to come see her. The other children lived near, they knew what she wanted. I was far away, and she hadn't had a chance to tell me.

The more she talked about it, the funnier it got to us children. She had told the minister what scriptures she wanted him to read; she had also given him a poem to read; she had chosen the soloist, the organist and the songs; she'd had her plot next to Dad's for fourteen years; she had had a good talk with the mortician, and made it plain to him she didn't want any money wasted on foolishness. She even asked us to be sure certain elderly friends had transportation to the mortuary. She led me to her closet and showed me the new dress she had bought for the funeral. She decided she didn't like the neck scarf, so she asked my sister to get another scarf "with a little pink in it." She asked another sister to let the hem down a little, and she asked me to get her some new underwear.

Next morning we sat at the breakfast table a long time, just talking. She was dressed and combed, of course, as she always was. Never in all my life did I ever see her eat breakfast in a robe. About noon she said she didn't feel very well, so I got her to lie down on the couch, though she resisted every step of the way. I sat on a footstool beside the couch and gave her some tea and toast for lunch, but before she finished it she dropped off to sleep. Later in the afternoon we realized she was not asleep, but in a coma. We called the doctor and an ambulance. She died three weeks later, never regaining consciousness, but as she had directed us many times, we did nothing to prolong her breathing.

During the funeral I remembered that night when she had told me just what she wanted, and I smiled to think how pleased she must be, to see everything going just exactly the way she had planned it. She died as she lived, with dignity, poise, gentle strength, and in complete control. She was a September woman.

OCTOBER. *During Balloon Fiesta everyone looks up and smiles.*

꓾

OCTOBER

When The Birds Go South

Some bright blue October day I hear the first sure sounds of winter, the purring, rolling call of the sandhill cranes going to their winter home at Bosque del Apache Wildlife Refuge south of Socorro.

Other signs of fall come a little earlier: aspen leaves have already splashed yellow on the north slopes of the Sandias; grasshoppers jump frantically and senselessly in the dry weeds and grass; there is a dusty pungency in the air, and the skies seem bluer than usual. Early morning mist clings to the ground, showing the ground is warmer than the air. But it never seems definite that fall is really here until I hear that first flock of cranes fly over.

Oh, the terrible wild freedom that rings from their call! It fills me with a longing for all the things I ever hoped for, and know I'll never find. The loneliness is as great and as empty as the sky itself. The sound lifts my spirit into an alien place, I feel part of the sky, the void, the forever where the wild birds fly. Their sound is primitive and urgent. It is part of the mystery of prehistory and of the distant future. It is a primeval sound telling man to go home, to find shelter. It is the sound of the seasons, the bittersweetness of fall and the joy of spring. It is as sure and as routine as the sun itself.

The sound also spoke to a poor, earthbound domestic goose in a farmyard pen near the ditch. The silly creature cocked his head, squawked, and flapped around the pen a few times. He knew he was supposed to do something, but he couldn't remember what. His run around the pen satisfied his migratory urge for the day. I wonder if the sound of the wild cranes told him that at one time his ancestors had flown high in the air for hundreds of miles with the sureness and confidence of a laser beam, and if the sound tugged at his primitive wisdom, it was an urge he no longer knew how to answer. He was content with his pan of grain and the secure fence around him. If he was missing anything, he didn't know it.

The cottonwoods in the bosque may not be as dramatic as the

aspens in the mountains, but they have their own special charm and surprises. Some years they drop their leaves without ever turning color enough to matter. Other years they turn from green to brown with nothing between. Then some years they turn slowly to a rich yellow canopy, covering the bosque with living gold. Their dark, gnarled trunks are like surreal pillars along the trails. Willows on the ditches and along the Rio Grande are a soft dusty pink. The water in the river is usually low this time of year, and it is often possible to walk across it without getting mud on your feet. One day we were walking up the river bed and two men on horseback passed us raising clouds of dust and, of all thing, a flurry of gulls. Who would believe such a story? A little farther along we saw a flock of several dozen Canada geese feeding on the bank. We played tic-tac-toe in the damp sand near a puddle that was the last remnant of flowing water, and noticed hundreds of silvery shad where they had been trapped in the quick-drying puddle, a coffin of curling river bed clay.

Another October day we saw a great blue heron wading in the ditch about fifty yards ahead of us, keeping the same distance, whether we stopped or walked, just like a kingfisher that swooped along the ditch, lighting on wires and tree limbs. A half dozen wild mallards flew up, making a great to-do about being disturbed. A muskrat dived under water and re-appeared fifteen feet downstream. Beavers had already begun to gnaw trees near the ditch, getting ready to build their winter dams. A cocky male pheasant strutted across the levee, making his raucous call so inappropriate to his beautiful plumage. Oh, yes, the bosque has plenty of charm in October.

In October, too, the more highly acclaimed, more photographed aspens put on a show in the mountains of New Mexico, forming golden cataracts tumbling down mountainsides. Some years it lasts for a week or more, other times the color is ended quickly by a hard freeze and cold wind. Colors of the aspens range from pink through apricot, orange, and golden yellow. Western sugar maples scattered in a few canyons of the mountains of New Mexico turn as startling a red as ever they turn in New England.

The balloon fiesta in Albuquerque is part of the mystique of October. Briliant, imaginative, no-two-alike orbs of color float soundlessly through the sky, as much a part of the fall landscape as the cottonwood, aspen or maple leaves.

Sometimes the balloons are low enough that we can speak with the crew. Sometimes they come lower than they mean to — like the Dallas balloon that got tangled up in the cottonwoods of the bosque and had to be rescued by helicopter. Or the time the crew from Finland ran out of propane and landed in the middle of Chuck Williams' horse farm. I had been watching them, and was there by the time the basket touched ground and the crew began crawling out. Surrounded by twenty or thirty excited horses, and approached by jeans-clad women from several directions, the poor pilot was sure he was in the middle of the Wild West. ''No shoot, no shoot'' he pleaded as we ran up to him.

Corrales Casa Tours used to be a regular event every October, to raise money for the fire department or library. We haven't had one for several years now, another custom that fell victim to the times. Too many people became too edgy about having so many strangers come into their homes. Too bad. Adobe houses, especially old adobes, seem more a part of the landscape in fall than at any other time. The soft brown color complements the yellow of cottonwoods and the crimson of chili ristras hanging from the ends of vigas.

Adobe houses hold a special place in the heart of true New Mexicans. This is more a matter of feeling than thinking. Adobe isn't so much a building material as a way of life, an attitude. It takes some people a few years to learn to like adobe, and some never do. That old line about ''warm in winter and cool in summer'' is true only if the house is built right. In spite of its drawbacks adobe is a natural, basic, unpretentious, honest material. Adobes have the handmade feel of a piece of pottery, especially in the old days when a house was replastered with mud plaster every year, often smoothed on by hand. Lines of an adobe building are horizontal and gently undulating, like the lines of mesas and sunsets. An adobe house comes from the earth; as long as it lives it is part of the earth, and when it dies it melts back into the earth.

In Spanish Colonial times building an adobe house was a family or neighborhood project. The mud was mixed in a shallow hole in the ground, with bare feet, sticks or hoes. Straw was added as a binder, bricks were shaped by putting the mud in a wooden frame, allowed to dry, then stacked sideways until cured. An adobe brick is usually from four to six inches thick, about a foot wide and from fourteen to eighteen inches long, and can easily weigh thirty pounds or more. Mud plaster was the same adobe mud without the straw.

From first hand knowledge making mud plaster is like making a batch of biscuits. You mix and add until it feels right. First you find the right kind of earth which has to have the right amount of clay in it. Along the ditch banks is a good place to find this where the mud has been dumped by the dredger. If it falls in blocks or chunks which crack, this is an indication there is clay in it which was deposited on the bottom of the ditch. Then you find windblown sand along fences and walls on the mesa, and with water add it to the clayey mud. Mix until it looks and feels like soft chocolate icing, take a ball of it in your hand and toss it a foot or so in the air. If it sticks to the palm of your hand, it has too much clay; if it crumbles when it lands on your hand, it has too much sand. When it is just right you can toss it several times and it holds its shape.

In the old days if a house had a foundation at all, it was a trench the width of the adobes, filled with rocks, which helped account for the undulating lines and the fact that nothing was ever plumb. As wind and rain tore away at the old adobes year after year, they eroded away just above the rock foundation, and eventually the walls fell outward. Now that they are covered with hard plaster and on cement foundations, this doesn't happen.

Indians built adobe houses before the Spaniards came, most of "puddled adobe,", which was one row of mud slapped on top of another, patted smooth, to the desired height. This method is really like making a pot by the coil method, where a coil of wet clay is wrapped around and around to make the size and shape of pot the potter wants, then pressed together and smoothed before it dried. I have an idea that this is how adobe houses started in the southwest. Some potter was building a pot one day, and said to himself/herself, "I'll bet I could make a house this way."

Adobe villages in the southwest remind people of adobe villages in North Africa and other places, but rather than it having come from one continent to another, I suspect people used whatever was at hand, and it was natural to use the clayey mud of the southwest to build with, just as it was in North Africa.

Corrales has its share of old adobe houses, though probably not as many as it might have if it were more isolated. Most adobe houses are not as old as people think, and sometimes say. If one survives two hundred years, it is remarkable and rare. It takes constant and tender care to help one last that long.

One of the older homes in Corrales was built by the grandson of Capt. Juan Gonzales, the Spanish don who bought the original grant from Capt. Francisco Montez y Vigil in 1712. Capt. Gonzales built a hacienda but the present house was probably built by a descendant in the late eighteenth century. Folklore has preserved tales of the Gonzales family, los *ricos* of Corrales Abajo. One Santiago Gonzales is supposed to have brought a beautiful silver bell from Mexico which hung in the *plazuela* of the hacienda. It rang when it was time to go to the fields, when it was time to come to dinner, and because the family were devout Catholics, it rang frequently throughout the day for the workers to kneel in the fields to pray. Stories say that Señora Gonzales also had a magnificent gold necklace, which, along with the silver bell, disappeared at the time of her death, and have never been found. The Gonzales hacienda now belongs to the Kruhm family and has been well-restored and preserved.

At one time the Gonzales property ran along the Rio Grande for a half a mile and extended west seventeen miles to the Rio Puerco. In the fertile valley land they raised fruits, vegetables and maybe a little *punche*, a native tobacco raised by most early settlers. On the mesa they ran thousands of head of sheep.

Part of the Gonzales property was sold to the Martinez family, and the central part of the village was called Martinez for many years. They built a big adobe hacienda where the restaurant, Casa Vieja, is now, though there is not agreement on when it was built. After the American occupation this house served as a court whenever the itinerant judge was here. The living room (main dining room of the restaurant) had a raised floor at the west end, originally used as the family *capilla* or chapel, which would also have served well as the raised area where the judge sat facing the length of the room. A little later in the nineteenth century this place was used as headquarters for the troops who came from Albuquerque or Santa Fe when the Navajos threatened or attacked the people of Corrales. An old cavalry sword was said to have been dug up on the property several years ago. The house was sold by the Martinez family in 1943 and has had several owners since then. Eleven of the original twenty rooms were restored and modernized, and the historic character of the house was kept intact. Since 1970 it has been a restaurant. The old house still has the grace and romance of the days when lovely señoritas twirled to the passionate music of the guitar.

Casa Imberte or Humberti or Miera — it has been known by all these names — is known now as the Rancho de Corrales, and is another of the older houses in Corrales. It was built by Luis Imberte, a Frenchman from New Orleans, sometime after the Civil War. He is supposed to have planted the first commercial orchard in Corrales which extended from the front of his house east to the river. An aura of tragedy hangs over this house, scene of six violent deaths. The deaths have become part of the folklore of Corrales, and details vary with every teller, but details don't matter much now. I like the way Lurlie told me about the first four murders:

Murder #1. "The Imbertes had a maid working for them named Lola. One day she was on a table in the sala, hanging grapes to dry for the winter, when the Imberte's spoiled twelve year old son came into the room and shot her for no reason. Maybe he was just playing and didn't mean to, but he should not have had a gun."

About murder #2, Mrs. Silva said: "One day Mrs. Imberte went to Santa Fe to see her lover. Mr. Imberte found out where she had gone and they had a big fight when she came home. That night she was sitting in the sala with a lamp burning. Mr. Imberte was outside, and he shot the lamp and kept shooting until he shot her."

The next murder plus two more related ones, took place during the ownership of the Miera family. According to Mrs. Silva, Pimenio Miera was a man of violence, but who often hired other people to do his dirty work for him. "Miera had one of his laborers to kill someone he was mad at, so when the time came for the trial, he had another workman kill the first one, so his part couldn't be proved." Mrs. Silva must have heard this story many times, for the details were so clear in her memory. "This killing took place in the big fruit cellar in front of the house which was filled in only about fifteen years ago. A nice green lawn and a big cottonwood tree cover where the fruit cellar used to be. Well, when this worker brought in some fruit to the cellar, the other guy hit him on the head then hung him from the ceiling by a red neckerchief he had around his neck. This would make it look like a suicide. His pants were rolled high, as he had been irrigating the orchard, and his shoes were muddy. He hung two feet above the floor at the entrance to the cellar, and there was a muddy puddle below him where his shoes had dripped."

"But that Miera got his reward," Mrs. Silva continued. "He made a loan to an American who was very sick in bed, and Miera told some friends he was going to shoot that gringo if he did not pay him soon. So one day he had a worker drive him over in his fine buggy to the gringo's house. Mr. Miera had on a white overcoat (linen duster), and when he got down from the buggy he took his gun and said, 'I'll get that gringo.' But someone had told the gringo that Miera was coming for his pay, and so he sat on his couch with his high powered gun. When Miera came on the path in front of the gringo's door, he was ready and fired. End of Miera."

But it wasn't the end of violence and tragedy connected with people who live in the house. After it became the Territorial House Restaurant two men tried to rob the owner one night. They pulled guns, and one shot the owner, who, nevertheless, was able to follow them outside to the parking lot where he shot both of them. One died, as did the owner.

Casa Gutierrez-Sandoval-Cordova-Krogdahl, northeast of the old church, is believed to be the second or third oldest adobe house in Corrales. It was started sometime after 1750 by the Gutierrez family, a family which had been prominent in Bernalillo since 1704 when settlers returned to the Bernalillo area after the re-conquest. The house is in the central portion of the grant, and grew with the family as was the tradition. As sons and daughters married, rooms were added, and the old adobe has stretched to accommodate many needs. The elasticity has continued to the present; it is now three homes with common walls.

The northernmost portion, an eleven room home, has kept the character of the original house, and some parts of it may be part of the original building. All walls are adobe, some more than thirty inches thick; floors are brick or soft pine (replacing earth and ox blood) worn smooth as silk through the years. It has six fireplaces, including one outside on the portal. The central portion of the house still has the traditional thick adobe walls, but has been changed considerably through the years. The south portion is the most recent addition to the venerable adobe.

These and a few dozen other old and well-loved adobe homes in Corrales have left a legacy of earth, sun and timber, of people using what was natural and easy, and learning to value it through time. Dozens of handsome new adobe homes are scattered along the ditch banks and mesas, and if they receive their share of tender care, they too will become part of the adobe tradition.

Adobe is as timeless as the Sandias, as much a part of the New Mexican landscape as the gnarled cottonwoods, and the apple-scented valley in October. The golden leaves and the crimson ristras of chili are the colors of the flag of Imperial Spain. No wonder those early settlers felt so at home here in October.

NOVEMBER. A *beaver dam raises the water level in Nicholls Drain almost two feet.*

∋ℂ

NOVEMBER

The Color of Siamese Cats

By November the cold nights have taken away the green of summer and the gold of fall, but rich colors remain. Willow bushes, bare of leaves, make a dusty cloud of pink along the ditches. Seed pods hang brown and stiff from weeds and grasses. Sometime during the month the field will be white with frost when we get up in the morning, covering the light beige of stubble with a thin white blanket. Soon the pale sun rises above the trees and mountains and wipes away the frost as if from a counter top. One of the Siamese cats stalks an elusive critter across the field and is lost in the browns and tans surrounding him.

Cottonwood trees hang grimly to the last of their leaves, rattling in protest. Each day a few more give up and flutter down like big brown snowflakes, but even when the new leaves come next spring, a few dry ones will still be clinging to the limbs. Bark and limbs of the cottonwoods etch dark random lines across the wintry sky, silhouetted at day's end by fiery sunset colors. This is November's impressionistic art, dreamy and imaginative. November is a time of waiting. The heat of summer and the glory of fall are gone. Passions are spent. The sharp energizing of winter has not come yet. November holds still and calm, breathing quietly with acceptance and remembrance.

All month the cranes and geese fly overhead. They come in waves, one wave not getting out of earshot until another appears over the northern horizon, calling their shrill call long before we see them. Sometimes they break and wheel, circle down as if to land, then continue south, responding to an instinct they do not question. I could not stop them if I built a wall to the moon.

Hummers, orioles and grosbeaks are all gone, but juncos and finches feast on the seeds that cling to dry weeds and shrubs. Some years a flock of Steller's jays comes in November for a few days, big, noisy, aggressive birds. They swoop into the Russian olive tree above the seed feeder, driving away all the smaller birds which return as soon as the jays fly off. The jays don't usually spend the winter in the bosque, but one year, for some reason we do not know, they stayed from November to May. There were hundreds of them throughout the valley, their metallic blue color a welcome addition to the drab colors of winter.

In late November or early December we make our annual pilgrimage to Bosque del Apache Wildlife Refuge south of Socorro. We have watched great flocks of cranes flying over for two months, yet we are always astounded at the thousands we see at the refuge. More than 57,000 acres of land along the Rio Grande have been set aside for them. Hills rise up on both sides of the river and bosque, barren and sere by day, but taking on the soft tones of crumpled velvet at sunset when the birds come back to the wetlands to roost. Along the river are cattail swamps, marshes, reeds, and dense stands of cottonwood, Russian olive and tamarisk. The flat irrigated fields are planted in millet, milo, and alfalfa on a cooperative basis with nearby farmers. They harvest two-thirds of the crops and leave the rest for the birds. Ditches wind through the fields draining them to make planting the rich bottomlands possible. Low spots stand in a few inches of water, creating marshes for the wading birds. Woods and brush border the east side of the refuge, providing habitat for many more birds and animals. Thousands of creatures spend all or part of the year here, but the highlight is during mid-winter when the sandhill cranes, snow geese and Canada geese are there in great numbers. A dozen or so whooping cranes, though, are the stars of the show. Whoopers have been almost extinct for years, but are gradually responding to a program to re-establish them. They stand over four feet tall and have a wingspan of more than seven feet, so their big white bodies are easily spotted among their slightly smaller, pearl grey sandhill cousins.

At sunrise most of the birds fly from the wetlands north to feed in the grain fields, and at dusk they return to sleep on the shallow ponds. Beginning around four or four-thirty they begin to appear on the northern horizon as thin, dark lines, wheeling and undulating, silhouetted against the evening sky. Wave after wave passes overhead, so low you can make eye contact sometimes. The geese honk and the cranes make a plaintive, purring "garoo-a-a-a" sound as they come in to their resting place and settle down for the night with a great deal of pillow talk.

We like to go down to the refuge early enough in the afternoon to walk some of the nature trails. We never fail to see deer, and more than one year we have watched coyotes stalk geese or ducks across the frozen fields.

It's always cold after the sun gets low, sometimes it's miserably cold and raw, and it's a long drive home, but we wouldn't miss it. We relieve the pain with a thermos of hot coffee, and maybe one of martinis, then we drive up to San Antonio where Conrad Hilton carried his first suitcase, and have the world's best green chili cheeseburger at the Owl Bar & Cafe.

November is when the beavers become most active. I don't know why — I'm a bystander, not a scientist. Along the ditches south of us they often cut fifteen or twenty trees a year, and build dams which raise the water level of the ditch upstream from the dam a foot or more. When we walk the ditches we see constant signs of their activity — gnawed trees, downed trees, tracks, places where they pull limbs across the trail and slides where they have worn a smooth path down the bank into the water. They are, indeed, busy.

Beavers can become a nuisance. Their dams sometimes back up the water in the ditches causing septic tanks not to drain properly, and adobe foundations to crumble. Their dens often cause ditch banks to cave into holes, a hazard for foot or horse traffic. One year they built a big den in the ditch bank bordering our property, with the main entrance, typically, under water level on the ditch side, and the back door where they come out into the woods to cut down trees on our side. Then when they built their dam downstream a quarter mile to raise the water level where they wanted it, it backed up the water so much that it flowed right through their den, in their front door and out the back onto our property.

It was a beautiful sight to wake up on a cold winter morning to find a frozen lake almost to our front door. A few more inches and the water would have been in the house. So we called Middle Rio Grande Conservancy District who called Game and Fish who trapped the beavers and took them away. But it wasn't long till we saw signs of more beaver activity, so they never get them all.

It's just a myth that beavers are such great engineers. They get the job done, but it's not precise. It's an accident if a tree falls where they need it. It just as often falls the opposite direction, sometimes across a levee. Beavers cut down trees for three reasons: to eat the soft inner part below the bark; to get limbs to make dams; and to keep their incisor teeth from growing in a complete circle and locking their jaws together.

Even though beavers are a nuisance, you can't help liking them, and admiring their industry. I'm always torn about calling for help when they get carried away building too many dams. The Middle Rio

Grande Conservancy District is the Godfather of the River, you know. They say when the water will flow, who will use it, and I even wonder sometimes if they have a direct line to God so they can tell him when it should snow up in Colorado. If I report the beaver activity, they'll have someone come trap and take them away. Even as late as the 1960s there was a beaver trapping season in the ditches north and south of Albuquerque, and the pelts brought a good price.

Mountain men thought they had them all trapped out by 1845, but there are probably more beavers today then there were then. Beavers will still be around, along with coyotes and cockroaches, when man blows himself off the planet.

November used to be the month when we had the Fireman's Ball. They have been held in barns, hangars and Perea's Social Hall. Annette Jones was often in charge, and when she was, things got done. She could get the biggest beeves, the most booze, the best bands and the biggest turnout. She sold tickets to the Mayor of Albuquerque, got contributions from companies that didn't care if Corrales dropped dead, and ads for programs that were lucky to ever be printed. Everyone in the village helped. We've come a long way since then. We now have *two* fire departments. How this happened is "pure Corrales" or democracy at its most inefficient.

When the village was incorporated in 1971 it included only the core area. The first mayor felt one way to force other areas into the village was to withhold village services to those outside the village boundary. The only service they had to withhhold was the fire department. This didn't set well with the people who had raised money to start the fire department, so Harvey Jones said, "By God, we'll start another one," and they did, big red trucks and all, with another Fireman's Ball. So now we have a Corrales Fire Department, and a Corrales Valley Fire Department in the same building, and as far as the naked eye can see, they get along fine. We haven't had a Fireman's Ball in years. We get state funding and probably grants of some kind, and grateful people sometimes contribute cash to the department. But most of the fire fighters are volunteers and when there's a bad fire the neighbors still help.

I remember one November when we had an unusually heavy snow storm for so early in the year. All day the wind blew snow horizontally across the winterscape. By night six or seven inches had accumalated and the temperature had fallen almost to zero. Snow clung in white crescents to the corners of windows like a Christmas scene, but the house was cozy and warm.

Next morning the storm had spent itself, the wind had died, and all was white, a world at peace enveloped in stillness. Juncos ventured down to the seed feeder, one or two at a time, sinking into the soft snow up to their chins. They pecked and scratched until they found seeds. I stood still against the window just a few feet away. As they pecked at the seeds I saw a miracle: their breath made wisps of steam in the cold air, and minute crystals formed on their beaks. How many mortals have seen the breath of a snowbird on a winter morning?

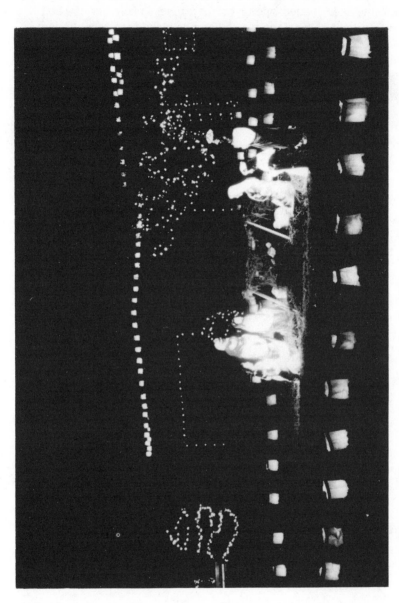

DECEMBER. Luminarias and Holy Family scenes make Christmas special.

꩜

DECEMBER

A Fullness of Heart Time

For all its cold starkness, winter is just as beautiful in the bosque as summer and fall. The sky is a pale silvery blue, limbs are bare and crooked, snow lies in patches under the trees. Storms are sharp, but don't last long. Sometimes snow changes to sleet with wind, howling and wild; then it clears, the sun comes out, and it is possible to go outside and sit with your back against a sunny wall and a take a siesta and listen to the birds. Winter birds are just as interesting, though not as colorful, as summer birds.

All winter the crows come every afternoon, cawing shrilly and steadily. They light in the trees and peck at dried Russian olives, making them fall like rain on the roof. The ground where the horses feed is black with them, picking up spilled grain. The cats ignore them, completely outclassed. Occasionally we see a pair of doves during the winter, laggards who never made it very far south. Scrub jays, Steller's jays and chickadees come down from the mountains for brief visits. Flickers, with their polkadot breasts, orange bibs and underwings, make a constant and reassuring flash of color through the barren trees. The resident kingfisher continues to swoop down from power lines to nab a morsel from the ditch. A blue heron that decided to stay here instead of going to the wildlife refuge stands like a statue in the shallow water, casting a sharp reflection in the barely-moving ditch water.

Some mornings there's land fog over the field, and a mist over the ditches, like breath rising from the water. It steals through the trees fleeing the sun which will quickly consume it. Sometimes frost hangs every tumbleweed, sunflower stalk and dried weed with white lace. As the sun creeps down the trees toward the ground, the frost disappears, and the weeds look dry and brittle again. If it has snowed a little I may walk farther into the bosque, to see if I can find rabbit tracks before they melt away. If a dusting of snow falls during the day, the Sandias will look like a strawberry-marshmallow sundae at evening. The late afternoon shoots golden rays across the bosque, lighting the tops of cottonwoods as if the light came from within the trees themselves.

December is a month like no other, not just for the natural beauty and wildlife, but for the tapestry of customs of three diverse cultures which are still important in our lives today, and especially precious at Christmas: exotic ceremonials of the Indians which they share with us; customs handed down by the Spanish colonial settlers whose life in New Mexico for almost four hundred years has left a permanent imprint on our minds; and customs remembered from Anglo pioneers who came by mule back, wagon train or boxcar. At Christmas each of these cultures is distilled to the essence of what makes it memorable.

One of our first Christmases in Corrales we went to see Los Pastores performed in Perea's Hall. I've forgotten who the characters were, but I'll never forget how blissfully Bortolo slept through the noisy cavorting and exhortations of Lucifer, dressed in long red underwear and carrying a pitchfork, as he tried to distract and discourage the faithful shepherds from finding the Baby Jesus. We have seen the play many times since then. It is performed almost every year in some village near Albuquerque, or in some community hall, or at the University. We still do Las Posadas in Corrales some years. Anyone who wants to join in is welcome to light a candle and hum along, even if they don't know the words. This play too, like Los Pastores, is done every year somewhere - in Old Town, Los Griegos, Los Duranes, Los Padillas, Alameda, Barelas.

One Christmas we went to visit the Cajero family in Jemez Pueblo. They had let us know they were having the shrine at their house that year. A winter hunting dance was going on in the plaza when we arrived, two clans alternating with the drummers and dancers of one clan coming into the plaza before the last one had entirely disappeared. There were three buffalo dancers, two men and one woman, about a dozen deer dancers, five eagle dancers and the singers. The exciting rhythm patterns and chants, and the flow of color and body movement mesmerized us in the bright winter sunlight.

When the dancers stopped we went to Cajero's house which was decorated on the outside with assorted Anglo decorations — evergreens, colored lights, a lighted Star of David and a nativity scene on the roof. But inside it took our breath away to see the decorations. A shrine had been set up at one end of the long living room behind an arch wrapped in Navajo rugs with jaclahs (turquoise necklaces) and other jewelry hanging from it. Statues of Mary and the Infant were on the altar where everyone who came in knelt a moment to pray, and to sprinkle a pinch of sacred meal over the Infant. John and Loretta were seated on either side of the altar in quiet, friendly dignity. She was in ceremonial dress - white leggins, moccasins, black manta over one shoulder, a white blouse with ruffled sleeves, and lots of jewelry. He wore his black suit. They greeted all guests who came into the room, and when he hugged me I felt a special warmth for this frail, elderly man whom I had known since we were both young and robust. Loretta was less outgoing, her handshake just a touch, not a grasp, but her eyes twinkled with warmth and friendliness.

The feast table was set up at the other end of the room and twenty-five or thirty people were eating. They came and went constantly. Benches were set up around the wall, and people had time to sit awhile before a place at the table opened up.

The ceiling was more beautiful than anything else. It was completely covered with fringed silk scarves, tacked so the fringe hung down, forming squares of colored silk. Over the altar, balls of cotton were hung like snowflakes, and dozens of egg shells painted in exquisite pottery designs hung by invisible threads. All the Cajero children were there — Cecilia, Margaret, Lucas, Joe, Frances, Carol, Tommy, Eleanor and Isabel. The girls were in ceremonial dress like their mother. Most of the children and their families live in Jemez, but one or two live in other pueblos or towns, but all had come home to help their parents host the Infant. The girls had helped paint the eggshells, and they and other female relatives cooked and served the food. There was mutton stew, red chili stew, turkey, sweet potatoes, canned peaches, biscochitos, pies, cakes, cookies, salads and coffee.

Each year a family is chosen to have the Infant in their home from December 24 to January 7 when it is returned to the church for another year. It is a great mark of honor and respect for the host family, but it is a tremendous undertaking to serve every person who comes to their house during that special time.

The fullness of heart I always feel a few days before Christmas is the culmination of what I feel about life these years in New Mexico. No matter where I lived whether it was Albuquerque, Corrales, Raton, Capulin, Las Cruces, Gallup or Santa Fe, it is part of the Christmas ritual. On the day everything is ready a deep feeling of satisfaction comes over me. The house is clean, the bricks glow, it smells of biscochitos, pumpkin and chili. I admire the dried sunflower stalk, the dockweed or the tumbleweed we sprayed silver to use as a Christmas tree. Yarn *huicholes* hang from them or a tin angel, donkey, star, owl, snowman or toy soldier. The Oregon holly someone sent is bright green and waxy with so-red berries; mistletoe we gathered from the cottonwoods in the bosque hangs in the middle of the ceiling, juniper and nandino berries are on the coffee table. What a crazy mixture. It wouldn't take a prize for a window at Goldwater's' but to me it is beautiful. I put a record of old-fashioned Christmas carols on the stereo, sit on the floor dunking a biscochito in a glass of wine, and think, "Hello, Baby Jesus. We're ready for you — all of us — Hispanic, Indian and Anglo."

We will light luminarias, we will go to a midnight mass, watch Los Pastores, join in las Posadas or go to an Indian Pueblo. We will put chili on everything we eat, and serve biscochitos and coffee to everyone who knocks at the front door. We will exchange Christmas presents and go to the Oratorio at the Methodist Church. We are suffused in history, part of the stream of people who have walked along the Rio Grande for thousands of years, carrying on their traditions and learning new ones as they come along.

Only in New Mexico, and especially in our little corner of the state, are we priviledged to feel part of the timeless flow of history, of the blending of whatever people have been here before us. Of earth and sky is our life made. To earth and sky it will return.